Love, Sex

and Aliens

Kamila Knapik

Published by Kamila Knapik 07/11/2013

ISBN: 0615730205
ISBN-13:978-0615730202

I dedicate this book to my beloved son Amadeus.

Tell the sun not to set
Tell the rain not to fall
Oh that kiss I think about

Contents

Chapter 1
The three stalkers

Yes, I did swallow their juice because I truly loved them. All three of them. Peter, Maison Boy Toy and Mr. Hazy. I guess that's why they still want me back and stalk me. Maybe they feel like I have that juice which belongs to them. You won't believe, but Peter, was a true alien, shape-shifter. Oh yes, he is still very motivated to have me back. He comes to me in different shapes of bodies. Oh, he was angry and power driven. Maison Boy Toy from South Carolina fell for my eastern European accent. Then again, I did fall for his southern redneck accent. Hellllooooooo. He was truly a sweetheart. Too bad none of his words were true. He could sell me the Eiffel tower from Paris and I would believe it was mine. The third one I drank his juice all the time every single time we had sex. Playboy-porn star, dark skin Mr. Hazy, with a big wily. A Creole from New Orleans, with a spicy mix of ethnicities which included black. He didn't even remember what he was saying the day after because he was smoking too much of the happy herb—marijuana.

I can't believe that I am talking so freely about my sex life. I guess my astrologer was right. Here it is, my advice to all you women; if you want a man to love you forever, drink his juice. Three out of three them. I always swallowed, and they keep coming back.

First one for six years, second for two years and the third one just 10 months now. They all three tapped my phone and hacked into my e-mail and my computer. And, they all three are not authorized for that. Quite oppositely, they tell me exactly what I have said over the phone. My best polish girlfriend, Nene, here in Florida, said that I must be very good in bed. I guess I am good. I am truly convinced that the juice in me is what makes them do that stalking.

The alien Peter was very amazing from the beginning. He was real gentleman looking. He liked to dress up and open the door for me. You know all the romantic stuff. Like flowers and long walks in the park. Gosh, I was crazy for him. He showed me extraordinary stuff. . . still I just wish he could stop drinking and be more suitable to people. But I know since he is not really from here, he felt he could find peace in me. And alien-shape shifter boyfriends, I guess they fall in love too! But I am a warrior soul. I do not surrender without a fight, even to aliens!

He opened my eyes to unlimited potential. He was my first big love of my life.

Maison, was the silliest one, I dated him only three months. When I found out that he was married, I stopped sleeping with him, and took back the copy of my house key that I had given to him. But he still went crazy and started breaking into my house several times when I wasn't there. I guess he was smelling my panties or something. He kept laying his business cards everywhere in my house. I had to get restring order against him, because I was scared of him.

And Hazy . . . he gave me the best sex of my life. Second biggest love of my life. I thought I was going to marry him. I never was so happy. But he dumped me because he thought that I didn't like his mom. Yet, his friend shows up at my house and he asked me how am I doing without Hazy? Good question, the sex was so good he literally open my Kundalini. Like I needed anyway, with all my third eye powers I have sometimes. When I was with Hazy, I was drinking alcohol and smoking pot. This clouded my psychic ability and I didn't have to see or hear crazy things. How would you like to dream about something at night and then the next day it was happening? Or dead people coming to you at night, while they actually died that night. Or seeing auroras of people around them all the time. I know it's crazy and I cannot really share this with everyone.

Deep inside me I feel that Hazy wants to propose to me. Tomorrow is his mother's birthday, and he wants to propose to me in front of his mother. Like it was his way he could prove to us that he loves us both the same way. God knows, I truly love him but he is such a mamma's boy. But Hazy, he's not going to propose to me tomorrow. Because he knows I have little flu and his mom has a cancer. Therefore, she cannot be exposed to bacteria like this.

I don't know, maybe it's all in my head. And I imagine that I might have a bipolar disorder and I see things around me. But I got my bachelor's degree at the University in Criminology and in minor in Psychology. So I must be smart somehow, somewhere . . . I studied crazy people so I thought I could understand myself better. Ha-ha. What a bummer conclusion. I came to the same point, like 20 years ago. I have opened my third eye, I am psychic and I see stuff like you watch on TV. Not every day though. Thank God, I learned one thing. When I drink and smoke, I have less and less of those crazy visions. When I am sober for months, it all comes back to me. I really don't like to be psychic because it puts me in a fearful position or illusion most of the times. I guess this is a gift and so called curse at the same time, and I have to live with it.

Maybe Hazy will to come to OZ this week, the ladies and gentleman's club where I have worked for the last 2 years as an exotic dancer. Like a real American dream girl. I have to dance to put myself through college. And on top of that, I am a single mom so it's all excused. As Hazy's mama says. I can cut my hours of work to only 20 hours a week and have more time for school and my son. Dancing at the club has also been very sensual and liberating for me.

Before I got pregnant with my son, I was a vegetarian, yoga teacher and transcendental meditation teacher for 10 years. I didn't have sex for almost 4 years in my 20's. Instead, I wanted to be an Indian nun. I was brain washed by an Indian guru named Sai Baba. One night, I had a dream where he told me to come for his 75th birthday party in India. In this dream, he invited me to be there, because he wanted to initiate150 future teachers by him. And he told me that it is great honor for me, because there are only 50 white people out of this 150. At that time, I was broke and living in Geneva Switzerland, working as a babysitter and as a home helper. I told that dream to a lady from the Sai organization where I was attending weekly meetings and meditations and she happily paid for my trip to India. She considered it a blessing that I had a dream of him. Is that crazy or what? However; later on I started to have sex while studying the Tantra techniques, which helped us achieve enlightenment thru sexual intercourse too, not only thru meditation and yoga.

When I got back to Geneva, I got myself a tattoo to remind me, that I don't ever want to be a nun in this life. I met this gorgeous Egyptian man that made a beautiful tattoo for me on my sexual chakra in the lower part of back. Which I find out, five years later in America, the tattoo's on girls located down there are called a tramp stamp. I didn't know that was so called in American culture, but what can I do? My tattoo is a little sun to represent the Egyptian God of the sun, Ra, and two dolphins inside the sun which represents a happy playful couple. On my sexual chakra like I said to represents that thru sex and relationship we can achieve nirvana as well. My tattoo is still there but I am still fabulous and single in Tampa Bay. The tattoo artist was such a handsome and sexy guy, that I had to take his invitation for dinner and breakfast. He got me a joint, but I hadn't smoked up in almost 10 years. OMG, I went crazy. I couldn't stop talking and laughing of course. But the sex was great. He liked my booty in particular. I didn't know what a wonderful pleasure that was. One of my favorites right now.

Hazy never wants to kiss me there. He just want have sex there and of course he wants me to drink his juice. He's very talented but a spoiled brat. Everything has come so easy to him because of his wealthy parents. I don't feel like he fully understands me. He is different for sure but he never has to hide like me. I don't know . . . He did porn movies with his mom, go figure. Well, they directed them together, that is what he told me. I don't know but for me, that is a little too much right there, of the son—mother relationship. I wonder what I am going to tell him when he shows up. I love him.

Back to stalker number two, Maison. When Hazy and I split, Maison showed up at my wonderful work place. He begged me to come back to him, he must have heard over the phone that Hazy and I had broken up. Maison had supposedly got divorced, so he wasn't cheating on his wife any more. He knew that I wasn't talking with Hazy over the phone any more. He is a nice and harmless guy after all.

Those new technologies over the phone are totally crazy. Right now everybody can listen to your conversations and read your text messages, only if they pay some money. I remember from my criminology classes, that this surveillance is a felony and can lead up to three years in prison. But who cares, married couples can do that to each other by law. And they can use this against you in divorce court. What a world. No privacy any more. Now all three of my ex-boyfriends listen to my phone calls. What a treat for me . . . But then again, the FBI is also listening to me.

Before I went to USF, I got my Associates in Arts at a local Community College and applied to the FBI to work as undercover agent. That was my dream job at that time. It was the reason I studied criminology and psychology, to become a criminal profiler. What a trip it was. My first contact with the FBI was from a community College professor who taught a Political Science class. I asked him if he knows someone from the FBI and I told him that it was my dream to become undercover agent. My first job offer came quickly afterwards when a man from the FBI came to speak to me and offered me a job in Miami to get into the Russian mafia as undercover. I learned to speak Russian back home in Poland, when I lived under the Soviet communist occupation. But I was too scared to take this job. I was so scared that the Russians might kill me and that my son would grow up without a mother. So I did say no. The second time that I got a job offer from the FBI, they wanted to send me to Brussels in Belgium and the European Union headquarters because I speak Polish, English, French, German, and Russian. But I was so in love with the United States of America that I did not want to leave for years to come. I still regret that decision now.

Soon after these job offers, I broke up with my alien shape shifter boyfriend and became a single mom with 2 year-old baby boy Amadeus. I still think the FBI listens to my phone conversations. So its four different people that always take away my privacy, all at the same time. This is crazy insane. For my third job offer from the FBI, they contact me at OZ, and they wanted me to work as undercover stripper in Washington DC or NYC where human trafficking was terrible now. Russian girls were being brought to the United States legally, but the Russian mafia was taking their green cards away and forcing them to work as sex workers. Again I said no.

I don't know why, but I think I am scared for my life. What if something bad happened to me? There would be no family to look after my son after I am gone. I am the only family he has here in the USA. I am also scared of commitment and responsibility. I don't know why, I really want to be committed to a job and responsible. I work hard and fight for my opportunities, but when I get close to achieving my goal, and then suddenly I don't want it any more.

I just realized this crazy pattern; I do over and over again with everything. I rely on new adventures. For example, on that my 34th birthday I went to New York City with my hot, hot 100% Polish girlfriend. Lidia is very blond, big boobs, and is the one of my best girlfriends. She visited from Geneva for four days and we had the time of our lives. We went to the Buddha Bar and tons of other clubs. But on my way back to Florida, after Lidia had left to go back to Geneva, I waited for my plane for four hours. I was bored so I went for a beer or two.

And then I saw him! Gerard Butler, that gorgeous Scottish hunk. I didn't even remember his name at first but I knew who he was. Filled with liquid courage, I went up to him and asked him for a picture. We took a very nice picture together, he was smiling so beautifully. We got into a conversation and he says to me:

"Where you from?"

"From Poland." I say.

"Where you flying to?" His smile was astonishing.

"To Florida."

He asked me which city in Florida and then suddenly out of the blue he asks.

"Do you want to have sex?"

I was so shocked. I froze not knowing how to answer him at first. And of course silly me, I then said no to him. But only because my plane was leaving in 10 minutes. This was not enough time. Instead I just touched him, with one finger and I said "You are so hot" I made a tztztztztz noise and I ran away.

What a Moron! I need to learn how to say yes to the good things that suddenly happen to me! Say YES like a man. Believe it or not I ran back to that place in two minutes after, but he had already gone. I thought, I just want a kiss with him. I still have a picture on my Facebook, and all my close girlfriends are jealous that I got to meet him and that he asked me to have sex with him. Hot like hell, sizzling, burning hot he was.

Peter, my ex-alien boyfriend, is driving me nuts. He keeps calling me, like 40 times a day. I met him 11 years ago in Geneva Switzerland at my friend's birthday party. He fell in love with me at first sight. He is very handsome. Blond and blue eyes, very educated, with a Bachelors in business. He is beauty and intelligence all wrapped up together. When we met, I was already engaged to my future husband, Robert and was waiting to move to the United States. Immediately, I liked him, but just like a friend. I was already in love. He asked me out several times, but I was faithful to my future husband. Peter and I have the same friends, so for the 3 months I when I was waiting in Geneva for my visa to the United States, Peter and I kept meeting up at my best friend's house. Peter had just returned to Geneva from St Petersburg Florida where he had graduate from College. Both parents were from Czech Republic but he was born in Bern Switzerland. At the time I was torn a little apart, I wondered why two great guys wanted me at the same time? Why did I have to make the choice? Why not, just the stronger guy wins me over? Oh I forgot, we don't live in the Stone Age any more. At that time I didn't know that he was an alien. While I believed in the possibility of intelligent life beyond the Earth, I wasn't really interested in this topic at all.

My favorite spiritual experience was when I a saw flying fairy above the trees in a little forested park. During an international spiritual convention in Krakow, Poland, but I swear on God I saw it. And I was not on any drugs! This was when I was a strict vegetarian and an Indian nun. During this period, it was fun to have the ability to see the colors of people's auroras change. All of our emotions, like anger, love, passion or others have different colors. Forgiveness is green, unconditional love is pink, and anger is red. As I was living such a pure lifestyle, this opened up a channel to my third eye.

I don't consider myself crazy. But I don't know why my brain makes me see this stuff. Having psychic abilities does not make a person crazy. More and more, scientists realize that this is just part of the human brain that science does not fully understand yet. For this simple reason, we cannot test these abilities or prove that they are right or wrong. Social psychology 101. Psychic ability is not defined because it cannot be tested or proved. And I know many people have same psychic experience like me.

I remember that night very well. I was staying at my friend Angelica's house in Nyon, Switzerland. Angelica is my very best friend whom I have known since we were nine years old. I thought I was dreaming and I saw this ball of light shaped like a tennis ball, flying across the sky at an enormous speed. It fell right on my forehead, right on my third eye. I should have felt a great pain from the impact when it hit me, but I didn't feel any pain at all. I woke up to find that my body was floating up in the air, like 50 cm or so, above my bed. It was like my body jumped from the wave of the impact of that fiery tennis ball hitting my forehead.

I fell back on my back, overwhelmed by the surreal—real dream, but then a couple days later, I learned about Kundalini initiations from the Sai Baba organization. Guess what, I opened a book on Kundalini initiations exactly on the page that explaining the highest level of cosmic initiation. At first, I thought "that's crazy!" the idea of a ball of light hitting you in the forehead. That was what exactly what had happened to me. This is the true story of the opening of my third eye.

My worst spiritual experience was with a lost spirit who possessed a guy I knew who worked as a bio-energy therapist. Even the ex-alien boyfriend never scared me like the possessed man did. After this experience I prayed to Jesus so he would protect me from bad stuff like this. And, it worked! I never saw a possession since. I went to him, back in Poland when I was 22 years old. Right after this terrible car accident I had that killed my boyfriend Tom and his friend Andre. I was driving the car when I had the accident. I wasn't drunk and I wasn't speeding but still it happened. After this, I was really depressed for years. My family tried to help me move on and told me not to blame myself. So I went to this bio-energy therapist to help me get rid of the depression and start a new life. He gave me some good energy, although I didn't know just what kind of energy he was giving. After several visits we became friends and he invited me for dinner in some restaurant next to a forest. This was in Glebokie Lake in Szczecin, where I was born. After dinner while parked in the car, he was just talking normally about something when suddenly his whole head changed to the head of a black man. Suddenly he had 15 dreadlocks on top of his bald head pulled back tight into a ponytail. I instantly started screaming out loud. Then, as the black man, he spoke to me.

"You have seen my real face" Ha-ha, he started laughing at me, "Wait when you see your real face, than you'll be really screaming."

His face suddenly returned back to normal. I started screaming again. It was dark already, and I was completely terrified. Somehow I asserted my will power and ordered him to drive the car to my home. I just wanted to get home safe. I fought to overcome my fear, the situation went back to normal and the guy acted like nothing happened. That was the worst spiritual experience of my life. I can hear what you think, but I know it was true. I thank God for saving my soul that day.

I remember later, I saw on TV a program about tribes in Africa where one voodoo tribe that bore the same exact hair style like lost soul had. I think the spirit that possessed the man was from this African tribe. Afterwards, I went to a catholic monastery to speak with an exorcist priest about what had happened to me. I wanted to help this guy, to get rid of that lost spirit. But the priest told me that only the man's family could help him get an exorcism and that the man had to also give permission to the priest. I wasn't his family and I don't think he would have given permission so I stopped right there.

My beloved Hazy only does white voodoo. His grandma also does voodoo, but not his mom. He told me that he put some white voodoo on me. I asked why, and he told me he put a spell on me as a gift for his penis, so I would always want his penis. I thought that he must be desperate to do stuff like this and then to even tell me about it on top of it. I heard that people from New Orleans, this is what most of them believe and do.

People still make prejudice comments about mixed ethnic couples. Wherever we went out, Hazy and I would hear nasty and sexual comments about my being with him. One time when we were at a restaurant, these white pretty girls sitting next to us said out loud to me when Hazy went to the bathroom.

"She sure is with him because of his 15 inch penis." —They all started laughing so hard at me. I didn't say anything because I was shocked. Always when I am shocked I just get paralyzed and cannot say anything. They were lucky though that I wasn't drunk, otherwise my response would have been totally different.

Another time in a different restaurant this drunken white guy says to us. "He must eat your pussy real good like a real dog for you to be with him." I really don't care anymore what stupid comments people make because I truly love him and I was the most happy when we were together. But Hazy kept testing my love. He kept testing whether I truly loved him or his parent's money. But he went too far with the testing.

Maybe it's all in my head and I am crazy because I think I am being watched. Ha-ha. I don't know why I'm laughing because it's not funny when a crazy person says to herself that she might be crazy. Life is a gift. And I'm grateful that I can count each day. It doesn't matter if the girl is rich or poor. She just wants her man to step up and show how precious she is to him. And yes, I want a real love like in the movie Titanic; but I don't want to die for it. I totally miss having sex with Hazy, he absolutely opened my Kundalini and I had cosmic orgasms which lasted for up to 20 minutes. I guess his white voodoo is working because I want his penis back so bad. I also miss his smile and he's little jokes. I really thought he was the one who I had been waiting for my whole life. The last time I saw him, he said "I like you, I love you, I have fun with you but you need to understand" What I didn't understand was that he is controlled by his mom.

I feel stupid, in a low emotional state, waiting and hoping that he will come back. On top of that, I wish that he comes with an engagement ring. What a lunatic I am, but he broke my heart and I cannot get over him. He is in my dreams all the time, like he never left. It's so hard to live without him in real life and but live with him every night in dreams. What a sweet fairy tale . . . Yes, I had one dream when he proposed to me and I said yes. But the ring he gave me was not in my style, *so I told him what I wanted, a ring in a square shape and he got that message really well.*

Chapter 2
Spiritual swinging

*Y*ears ago, when I lived in Geneva, I was relaxing and lying down on the grass in a beautiful park just looking up at blue sky and watching puffy white clouds passing by. Suddenly I heard a loud voice, "You and your special man have to be both specially prepared because you both have a special mission."

What? I have a mission? Cool . . . I was so shocked, but when I looked up around me, nobody was there. I remember it was upsetting to me because this loud voice said the word "special" three times. This was the exact words I heard. It was just me and the nature. I have had a ton of vision in nature. The most important visions always happen in nature for me. I now understand that Chi energy, part of planet earth, is so pure and strong, that it becomes easier to connect with your own energy when you are relaxing in nature. No distractions, like a clean channel that is not polluted by smoke and alcohol.

I can feel it now; a women's revolution will be coming soon. Maybe it will be a sexual revolution, and Hazy and I will find out exactly how to open Kundalini channel like in the Tantra philosophy from almost 5000 years ago. And we can start having sex and levitate and we can activate Siddhi powers as well. This is crazy stuff according to Hindu philosophy. This could be very dangerous when you don't know how to use and control your Kundalini powers. You can spontaneously combust from the sexual energy and opening.

I know those powerful American lesbians will read this book and start practicing Tantra sex more than before. That would be awesome if they start levitating while having sex taking the consciousness of human beings to a collective new level. This new sexual tantric revolution could soon happen and overlap the critical mass.

When I was baptized in the Polish Catholic church, the priest didn't want to give me Kamila as my first name. He only said he would give me Kamila if my parents agreed to give me the middle name Maria. My mother agreed to this, and on my confirmation, I took the name Magdalena. Again a priest warned me of the name Maria Magdalena

"Do you know who she was?" He asked me. For me she was the closest person to Jesus after his mother. The priest was very much upset by my decisions. He told me, "Look at you. You are not only Kamila, the highest priestess of Isis, but also Maria Magdalena the prostitute; I wonder what your life will bring you . . . ."

I was just 15 years old and I did not have a clue what he was talking about, but I remember that conversation very well because he got very upset. At the end he told me that I had the power to change my destiny if I believed. I know now, exactly what he was trying to protect me from. I believe I can change my destiny, my karma. I am changing the destination of my life, right now. Moving to a bigger, better, brighter future, filled with love and prosperity now and forever more. I believe this is possible.

This happened in 2003 in France in a small village right next to the village where Joanna d'Arc was born. I was at a International Yoga Teacher Training course from Sivananda holy line, for four weeks. We slept in tents in the woods. OMG the ants were biting me for a whole four weeks. It was a nightmare like in military camp! We had to wake up at 5:00 am and study yoga the whole day. We also studied the Hindu philosophy of Ayurveda, Vegetarianism, and Meditation. My favorite was the meditation. We were taught by Indian and European monks. One of the teachers only lectured about Siddhi powers. He posed several questions to all of us, asking us to search our psychic powers through our third eye for what we could see and hear. I was the only one who answered yes to all his questions. Most of the people could only answer some of his questions.

After the class, the Siddhi teacher told me that I should only listen to myself and not to follow others. I should always know that is the best for me. He then called me the most psychic of all the 80 attendees. Since they were already spiritual people. Funny when I think of that because he was African, because at this point I hadn't met too many black people in my life. I saw his aura. He was all in pink. He filled the whole room with his beautiful pink energy.

The inspiration I gave to others comes from my experiences in my past's lives, but this life I need to inspire myself and focus on my creativity. This is exactly what is happening here. For now I am totally obsessed with myself and my name Kamilah. In Egyptian this name means "The Perfect one." Kamilah was the first woman who was allowed to praise the Egyptian Goddess Isis. In astrology I am an Aries, and in Chinese astrology I am a Tiger. The combination of an Aries and Tiger together, is the incarnation of the ideal woman. Again Perfect . . . . This is funny to me—the idea that a Sunday school teacher and exotic dancer can be the ideal woman. Or so the astrologers say.

I have a weird obsession about a little Hindu guy who keeps showing up at different stores. He always comes so close to me that it's like he wants to be seen and remembered. I remember Hazy once told me that the same guy was following him too. So weird. I met him again last week at the auto store. He asked me—"Where is that the third guy? He should be here already." I knew instantly that he was talking about Hazy. But I'm still waiting for Hazy to come back and take me to forever and more. One of my dear friends told me that Hazy and I look like Belle and Beast from the fairy tale, The Beauty and the Beast. I don't know about that, because he is not a beast. She explained that it's because of his mocha skin color and that we both look so beautiful at the end.

I had a dream three nights ago when Hazy won six million dollars in his lawsuit and he gave me one million dollars in $1.00 bills. OMG, it's like a stripers dream come true. I think I want to go to a swing house just for fun, just to see what it is like. Hazy knew the best one in Tampa where you have to pay $150 per person, but we only talked about going.

My maiden name was Blawat. Blawat means cornflower. Kamila is also the core word for chamomile. Field of cornflowers and chamomile growing together are beautiful. It is a name representing wild beauty and tranquility. I know I was told, that I am too honest with people. I understand this but I'd rather know the truth then be lied to by others. I can't help it. In my real life I absolutely have to be honest and real. I don't feel like poisoning my heart and my body with lies. I don't want to play that game. No thank you. I know you could see me, just as an exotic dancer and that you are judging me for what I have done but I wasn't born a stripper. Perhaps that Polish priest was right that I should have chosen a better name than Maria Magdalena. Could this name have actually messed up my whole life? I wonder if I had a different name, would I have a better life? I thought Maria Magdalena was Jesus' bride at the wedding where he turned water to red wine. There's a whole theory, about it than they have a daughter together. Her name was Sarah and they lived together as a family after resurrection in India. It was Sarah's children who immigrated to Europe and started the holy blood line of Europeans Kings.

Edith, a Master of Reiki, was good people and she could heal people for real. She could psychically see a lot of stuff too. I invited her for a dinner with my family and in front of everybody, she starts talking about my past incarnations. Like for real? Thank you girl. According to her, I was incarnated as a soldier when Jesus was here. That's why she said my soul got enlightenment so quickly. The strong aura energy of Jesus does that to people. I was born pure and one with light in this life. I guess it must be true, the energy is a key and never dies.

Edith said that I need to help my family's soul from their past lives. I took my sister Margret, my first cousin Michael, and my mom's heavy karma onto me in this life time. For all of my life, I have been heavily loaded with their karma. Now that I am 38, my real life is about to begin. I wonder why now is the time and if it's possible. In my new life, I think about sexual women's revolution and about energy sources. I think that the source of all energy is love. This is magical energy because love is magical. When I used to meditate, I often had the feeling of levitation, like my soul was lifting up. Love and sex has that energy too.

But that's not only it, even this new life has its problems and even now, I pollute my body with alcohol and smoke. And pollution comes from many other places. Recently, at OZ of course, they put air conditioning so low, that everybody is freezing there. Especially, when the girls don't have much clothes left on. Ha-ha. We dance only in bikinis, sometimes we might have stockings on too. So I always when I get to work, I change the AC temperature for 2 or 3 degrees higher. Last time when I was trying to change the temperature, I reached up my hand to push the button up and it changed by itself. I didn't even touch the button! I think that I must have spontaneously changed the temperature mentally somehow. When it happened, I told Hazy about it, I was so upset and crying I asking myself "What is wrong with me?" He hugged and kissed me, "Nothing is wrong with you baby" He said. He was so comforting and filled with love that day to me. Thank you so much my darling.

Back in Poland, I attended a spiritual workshop deep in a forest. There was a speaker from New Zealand who talked about fulfilled and healing relationships. I also wanted to clean my system at the time, so I fasted for that one week. I drank only water, fresh squeezed orange juice, and chocolate milk. It was the best fasting experience ever. In the forest, I felt so light while I walked. I had to look down, to see if I was walking not floating. Some Hindu books explain this is due to Kundalini raising or else maybe my alien, ex-boyfriend at the time was just doing some experiments on me that I don't even know about.

When the Kundalini wakes up thru sexual intercourse, the human brain can open up and be activated to psychic power. Aliens know how to do this to our bodies. It would be nice, if they could come down to Earth and show us how to open 100% of our capacity for sexual fulfillment and of course the brain too. Personally, I think the aliens would like to live among us and help and guide humanity towards peace. Crazy, I know but true. They live among us already, about 6 million of shape shifters. Supposedly they really want to be friends and lived here among us here and now.

Humans have this capacity too, I know this. I would also love to have my brain fully at work. And flying, why not? It looks like fun, fun, and fun. I love the star Angel from the Las Vegas Show. He is the best example of what humans can do when we learn how to harness our energy to improve and control our bodies.

We really don't fully understand the psychic capacity of the human mind. Or else, for those people who have learned how to tap into their powers, we don't know how to prove it that their actions are real. But those of us who are psychically strong and willing to try, we are ready to change the world. This can be achieved through the bliss of good sex too. We don't all have to meditate and become monks to accomplish nirvana. We are a very progressive society right now; only with this acceptance can Kundalini wake up. I am on my mission to make it work! LOL, what a mission? But I know it is possible.

I miss my baby Hazy. I know he opened my Kundalini. So much pleasure can come from being in a secure relationship. He is the one. I love him so much that I would even become a swinger and marry him at once. I think. Or maybe just marry and swing later. Ha-ha.

Chapter 3
Alien-human life

Anyway it's time to match up with facts. Hazy dumped me two months ago because I was according to him, complaining too many times about his mother not liking me. She was very sweet to me for the first three months but she started to scream right into my face and this scared me. She says that she sees a black energy in his aura since he started dating me and she doesn't like the weird lights floating around my head. Yes Hazy has black spots in his aura, but this is because he smokes too much pot and this is starting to sicken his aura and his body. But this is not my fault. Not my choice.

I was even more scared of how Charlotte, Hazy's mother, ruled his life. She would make all the most important decisions for him. On one hand I understand she just wants to protect him. She is worried that, I working as an exotic dancer just want to take his money. Hazy asked me many times if I was willing to sign a prenuptial agreement if we got married. I said yes, because I love him so it's doesn't matter to me. But that wasn't enough and he kept changing his mind. He tried asking his mother for money for an engagement ring for me, she wouldn't agree to this, Hazy said that he doesn't want to start the marriage without his mother's support and he tells his mother everything! As the distance between his mom and me grew, it became too much and he dumped me.

Nevertheless, I haven't had sex for two months now and I am going back to being very sexually frustrated. Go figure being a dancer. This guy was very handsome 6, 4 feet tall. OMG I love tall guys so much. He kept asking me out, so I agreed to go to dinner with him. We went for dinner at a French restaurant. After dinner that crazy lunatic showed me his ID and his last name was Cooper the same last name as the guy who Hazy was suing for his building. I freaked out and told him that we couldn't hang out anymore. That's when he threatened me to my face. He told me to stay out of Hazy's court case or I'll lose my eye. He literally threatened my life while we were on a date. I was so scared. But that wasn't the first time where I was threatened because of Hazy. One day we went to a Laundromat, and I left the door open in my car. When I went back outside to the car there was big piece of brick on the passenger seat where I had been sitting.

Hazy's friend talked to me at OZ the week before this weird situation happened with Cooper. That I should look forward to next Friday and that it would be very big day for me. I started hoping that Hazy would come and proposed to me or at least we would get back together. I think this crazy Cooper, heard Hazy's plans over the phone since he taped his phone too. Of course I told Hazy about the threat against my life. He even sound more terrified than me. So it's like, we have to live in fear now? I refuse to live in fear. Hazy thinks we cannot be together because of this sick, sick man who threatens us both. But I know we will be together sooner or later. I have been told this will happen, and I know it's true.

Hazy told me right away when we first met that he was in the middle of the court case for his building. The law suit is for about three million dollars. Hazy claims that a guy faked his signature on a contract and took away his whole building. This man was also throwing bricks at his building windows and at his house too and now into my car. Some people here in the south are still very prejudice and Hazy's building was the first business in downtown St. Petersburg with African American owner.

I know how terrible prejudice is from my own experience. My name is Kamila Knapik, last name after ex-polish husband. When I applied for a job in local Yacht Club, I think the fifth oldest Yacht Club in USA where the wealthiest people are the members. The new manager told me that they hired me because of my perfect alignment initials KKK and because I was blond and blue eyes. Isn't that very nice of them. So racist. Sad but true story.

I remember I had that dream about Hazy and his money. When I was moving out to my new place, I found a key to my house right in the middle of my living room. Of course Hazy had a key to my house before. Next to the key there were those 3 Chinese lucky money coins that he had showed me before; I remember them because I have the same coins from my mama long ago but with different colors. Hazy got purple ones and I got red ones. So now I have 6 coins together. I think he tried to send me a deep message by leaving those coins. I think he knew that if I had my 3 coins plus his 3 coins this totals 6 and this will lead to me winning $ 6 million I was dreaming about. I told him all off my secrets so he knew how to send a message to me.

Next to the key and coins was a card with the picture of the bear. That wasn't hard to understand at all. A while ago, I had other dream that Hazy and I were in this huge house with its very own private library. We were walking through the rooms, admiring the beauty of the house when suddenly we saw a rabbit, a raccoon and a big bear. The bear started to walk towards us. I screamed and started to run away. As I ran I lost Hazy, but in this dream he called me, asking "Why did you run away and left me alone with this bear?" He became mad in the dream, and in my dream he said this was really why we were not together, because I had left him when I ran from the bear.

I told my girlfriend about this dream, so I think he heard about it over the phone. He thinks that Cooper was the dream bear because he was so tall and that is why he left the card with bear. Sometimes, I wonder, "Do I really hear what I am saying?" but the funny part is that I essentially believe this is true and this is the real reason that we are apart. I sound like a crazy person, but I am tired of denying my psychic gifts.

I remember when I was leaving to America to marry Robert, Peter told me, "Too bad you didn't give me a chance, but you will get you're a green card and soon after you will divorce him."

"What are you talking about?" I said.

"While I want you now, it's better this way because then I can get my own green card from you when we eventually marry."

I thought he was crazy at the time, but in 6 months I was back in Geneva. Robert and I had gotten married; however, he started drinking nonstop. I should have known about this before we got married, but I had met him on the Internet, where we were friends for about one year before we actually met each other. In real life I knew him only two months, so I didn't really know him as well as I thought. I told him that I didn't like his drinking, so I would go back to Switzerland if he didn't stop. Instead of stopping, he pulled a gun on himself and tried to kill himself. He had been so drunk that he didn't even remember doing this the next day when he sobered up.

This was a sign to me. I thought I don't want to be killed by some drunken guy, who will not even remember pulling out and playing with a gun. Finally, after four months of marriage Robert's mother gave me $2000 and she said to me "You deserve a better man than him. Here is some money and go back to Europe and be happy."

I was so scared, so I took my ex-mother-in-law's money and come back to Geneva. Robert begged for a second chance for the next 8 months. He promised that he would stop drinking for good. But still I wasn't sure what I wanted. I wanted a divorce, but Peter, being my friend now, told me to go back to America and give Robert a second chance. Peter also told me to get the green card. I only had one year left to qualify for the papers. I was torn.

Then one night on Geneva Lake, I suddenly hear very loud voices. "Peter is coming your way." I looked around and no one had spoken. Yes, so nice to hear voices in my head again, I thought. A minute later Peter showed up next to me and then my dear friend Angelica showed up shortly after. I have known Angelica for 30 years now and she is my best friend forever. We are like soul sisters. One day when I was in park in Geneva I was just walking picking up some flowers. Suddenly I saw right before my eyes Angelica having car accident. I didn't want to believe this vision, because it had happened while I was awake. Usually my visions only happened while I sleep. Not believing myself, I ignored my visions, but only 10 minutes later she called me on my cell phone, "Kamila, I just had a car accident 10 minutes ago. I'm still in shock, so I need someone to talk to before police will come here."

"Angelica I just had a vision of you having car accident. I think I just saw it at when it was happened to you."

We both believed this. We have a very strong soul connection so I was able to see what happened to her at that exact moment.

Finally, Robert said that he wouldn't wait for me any longer and that I needed to give him an answer. To help me decide, I signed up for a 4 week Yoga Teacher training course in France. Robert paid for this. After this spiritual search, I promised to give him my final answer. I got my certification of yoga teacher but it was hard work. During that training the mother of one my friend Monica, got really sick and she lay in coma for couple weeks. Monica, ask me and my mom to send her mom Reiki—healing energy. It was like sending golden light across the distance. My mom and I both sent Monica's mom energy for coupled weeks. Then I had a dream with her mother. In the dream, she was thanking me for the light energy, and she asked me to help take care of Monica I woke up next day and called her, she told me that last night her mom just passed away. I called my mother, to tell her, and she said "I know already, she came to me last night in my dream too. She told me to take care of Monica." It was the same dream as I had!

I didn't have any visions with Robert so I made my decision I will give him a second chance. He stopped drinking for eight months and we had a very nice time together. But of course it didn't last beyond that. Robert started drinking again, we stopped having sex, stopped sleeping in the same bed. It was like he gave up on life. I wanted us to go to marriage therapy but he didn't want to. Instead, after three years of marriage we got a divorce. There was no drama at all and we are still friends today.

I was now 32 years old and wanted to have baby so bad. My motherly instincts were taking over. I started to wonder about Peter from Geneva. What would happen if I had chosen him instead of Robert? Peter was working at United Nations in Geneva at that time and was making great stride in his career. One afternoon I went to St Petersburg beach, here in Florida, to relax and read a book next to the water. In just a few minutes this tall and handsome man sat down next to me and starts up a conversation. His voice was so soft. It was the most hypnotizing voice I'd ever heard. I told him this. He responded to me "That's why I choose this body for now. I knew that you would like it. "I looked at him like he was crazy, "Man what are you talking about?"

We were sitting right near the water; unexpectedly we heard a real loud noise. It sounded like a jet ski but nothing was there. I asked him.

"Did you hear that Jet Ski?"

"Oh, Yes I did."

"What was that?"

"Maybe that was aliens using their invisible technologies to fool around with people like you. We do it all the time, for fun mostly."

"Yeah, right. Like I believe that." He invited me to a restaurant and over dinner he told me that he was married and had two kids. So I left and never saw him again. That was an unusual meeting.

One night after, I was out for drinks in downtown again with my polish girlfriend Lidia. We were just walking to next bar. I swear I saw Peter sitting on the corner with his guitar. This Peter had a long gray beard. I gave him a dollar and he smiled at me. I swear he was Peter, so I asked him. "Peter?"

"No, I am Charlie."

I was so confused. I couldn't stop thinking about this guy. Next day, I went back to the same place and there he was still sitting on the corner playing his guitar. I sat down next to him and we start talking.

"I know somebody who looks exactly like you just without the beard. He also plays guitar."

"I know you do, because I know you too."

I didn't know what to say about this comment. I just turn my head around too look somewhere else. When I turn my head back, he looked different already. Suddenly, he was bigger and older, having quickly gained 200 pounds. I was petrified.

"Do not be scared." he said, "I'm Peter and I can prove this to you." Well, what a trip I thought. I should run away from him, like right now. But then, I thought let's play his foolish game. So I asked him to tell me exactly where and when I met Peter.

"I met you first in France in a restaurant on our friend's birthday party."

This was exactly the truth, it was so disturbing to me. Peter as he shape-shift to Charlie's body started to talk about his life in Geneva and when we knew each other there. Then he told me that he was an alien. He explained that he was a shape shifter, and that he wanted us to be together. He couldn't be in two of the same bodies at the same time, and he also couldn't leave his political career in Geneva right now, so he took a risk and approached me in a different body. He knew that I was spiritual and accepting, so he trusted that I would recognize his soul in whatever body he occupied. I couldn't stop listening to him.

Of course I didn't believe him at all at first. I thought it was some kind of sick joke. But Charlie knew so much about Peter and I when we were in Geneva, including very small details that nobody else could know. I wanted to know more, so I invited him to my apartment to continue this discussion.

To prove that he was an alien, he showed me how to make stuff materialize right in front of me. For example, we were sitting in a kitchen and food just kept appearing suddenly in front of me. I know it sounds strange, but that is what happened. Although I didn't find him physically attractive, I wanted to know more and more about him. His face, voice, and the way he moved all reminded me of Peter movements. I wanted to believe that he really was Peter. After the food stopped materializing, the next trick he did was to make my dog Eddie teleport. One second he was in front of me and the next second he moved Eddie 10 feet away from me. I was amazed. He did promise to me that he would return to his Peter sexy body soon but for now he has to stay as Charlie.

Then he shocked me further, when he asked me why I had left him alone in that restaurant on the beach a couple days ago. "I wanted you to know the truth about me because I love you so much. I have been waiting for you for the last four years. I want you to understand me because I know you are capable of that."

He explained to me how supreme aliens mixed up their DNA with chimpanzees at first by having sex with them. As more and more alien DNA was added, because aliens male haven sex with us all the time. A new species emerged—today's human beings. Peter/Charlie explained that humans were able to do many things beyond our imagination. We just don't know our powers yet. He claimed that about six million alien shape shifters live on planet Earth now. They all look like humans and go about their lives mostly in the USA and Europe. For some reason there are more male aliens, and only a very few women aliens. He said that female aliens will not come here till everything is ready. Maybe this is why they had to keep mating with human women. He also said that his home planet is very cold and is dying. The aliens were looking for a new planet to live on, and decided they liked Earth. Many religions believe that aliens are gods. He said there are good and bad aliens, just the same like people.

Peter/Charlie and I began a relationship that lasted 3 years. At the end of it I was a mess. Therefore, to clear my head and focus on something else, I went back to University for my bachelor of science.

I think FBI listens to my phone still because of Peter/Charlie. He still calls me all the time, even though 5 years have passed. I don't know if I am crazy or just my life is crazy. I don't know why these things keep on happening to me. I felt for a long time that I had to keep this all inside and I couldn't tell anybody. I worried that people would think I was insane. But then I realized that I needed to write this all down for my own peace of mind. I can't hold this inside me any longer.

My opened third eye could be the reason for all of this. My visions started when my fiancé died in car accident. I was the driver, I wasn't drunk, wasn't speeding, it was just bad accident. Two cars smashed into each other and two people were dead. Tom and Andrew were their names. May their souls rest in peace. I was just 21 years old, back in Poland. Tom, my first fiancé, on the day of his funeral came to me in a vision to say goodbye. I was reading a book with the night lamp behind me. I was tired so I wanted to go to sleep, so I turned off the lamp and closed my eyes. In the same moment, through my close eyes, I saw beam of light from behind, pointing up to my nose. I open my eyes, looked behind me but nothing was there. When I closed my eyes again, I saw Tom's head appear but he looked like he was made up of transparent white smoke. I wasn't scared at all. He touched me with his warm hand on my cheek and he smiled at me. He had very happy eyes like I never seen before, full of love and happiness. He kissed me, and then he disappeared. I could feel a surge of unconditional love from him. I knew that he was happy. After that, I couldn't sleep whole night.

I think this first paranormal experience opened the door to the other side. Since then, I have had many visions. I remember one dream at night with a bio-energy therapist taken over by a lost voodoo spirit. In my dream he became red dragon. He was trying to kill me but I became a blue dragon. We started to fly and spin around each other in spiral. And I won.

I think my father was incarnated as a Dolphin before. For this reason, dolphins call out to me every time I see them. They say dolphins can hear and understand our thoughts, so when I was in Miami Florida for the first time, I decided to experiment little bit. I tried to talk to them in my mind while standing next to a pool before the show. I said to them, "If you can hear me please, come up to me right now." Right that second, 10 dolphins swam right up to my face in the pool. I started laughing so hard, I was so happy. They splashed water on me too. This was one of the happiest experiences of my life. I love dolphins very much, they are wonderful creatures.

Right now, I am sitting at home alone. I am a 38 year old woman with a smoking hot body and I haven't had sex for three months now. I am doing this celibacy for myself again. Go figure. Hazy is the man of my life, and I don't know if he is coming back to me. I don't know if he is really scared of the threats against our lives? I don't know if he is just waiting for his money? I am so blindly in love that I'm not seriously considering that he might not want me anymore. Ha-ha.

Oh well, we will see what the future brings. I really don't know anymore, maybe I am just sweet crazy and imagine stuff in my head that I think will come true. I know I am really good at doubting and denying myself in everything. However, I have learned to use it as my defense shield because if I don't believe in something and deny it at first, then if it becomes true that means that I am not crazy imagining stuff. Also I won't be disappointed if my dreams don't come true.

Coming back to my dreams. While I was in Montpellier France, during the summer of 1996, I lived on a small hotel boat and I got this extraordinary vision. I was at the beach relaxing when I saw myself, flying out of planet Earth. In space I fly through three white tunnels that look like spirals. I came to a place that was totally white and I looked around me. I said to myself, "God where are you?" I felt so close to God at that time. I couldn't stop wondering why this was happening to me. Had my Kundalini woke up, was this from my third eye? Or were aliens doing some of experiment on me?

My trip to India was nice. The first time I went to India was to see my guru Sai Baba. As soon as I got to the ashram I started a period of silence, not talking for two weeks. I carried with me a small notebook to write to people if I had to communicate. I didn't realize the significance of this experience until it was over and I started speaking again. After the two weeks, when I first started speaking to my friend, I literally saw pink energy, like a little cloud, coming out of my mouth. Pink is the color of pure love. This showed me how every sentence we speak is so important.

I think I know finally why I studied criminology and psychology. I wanted to know if I'm crazy. According to an Abnormal Psychology textbook I could have a Schizotypal personality disorder. People with this disorder typically have socially isolated lives and behave in ways that would seem unusual to others. They tend to be suspicious and have odd belief. Yes, this sounds like me! Another example from the book is the "Man with the mission" -who claimed to have opened his third eye and being a vegan. For this he was called crazy. In the same book, they described the most famous astrologer who was foretold about his glorious future by a psychic friend as an example of the unknown capacities of the human brain.

I studied for six years in college. All these smart books and I feel like I didn't learn what I wanted to know. I guess it's true when they say if you learn and learn more, you feel like you know less and less. It is so hard to prove metaphysics. But then again, I don't want to prove anything to anybody. I just want peace of my soul.

Right now I feel like I'm constantly being watched by my two ex-boyfriends Maison and Hazy at my work place. I think they sent some of their friends to talk and keep track of me. Hazy once told me "I know what you doing there at OZ, they told me exactly what you do, but I understand because that pays your bills."

The second example is when they using technology to track me. They can put the virus to your smart phone and they can listen to everything that is going on around you. It's like a microphone that sends everything to their email and computer and the other phone also. So basically they can hear you 24 for 7, even when you are not on the phone talking. But if you take the battery out, the microphone stop working, so I did took my battery out when I went for that dinner on that date. I didn't want Hazy to know or to hear me, if I decided that I wanted to have sex with that crazy Cooper. The next day at OZ, this guy came up to me, and said to me "Baby don't worry, nobody can hurt you. Do you know why? Because you see that guy" he pointed at my manager, "he's watching you like a hawk. Like a hawk, can you hear me?" he was very threatening and pointed at his friend who he called policeman. "He wants to tell you something."

The policeman so called friend came over, and he took his cell phone out, "You see this, this is cell phone. "He then smacks me on my face. I was so shocked. He said "Do you understand?"

So basically, I was slapped on my face by some stranger, who was probably an undercover policeman, for taking my battery out of my cell phone in my attempt to stop them from hearing what was going on during my date. I don't know if that was coincidence but again I don't believe in coincidences at all.

Sure the Military or FBI could hire me as help for a future alien invasion since my ex-boyfriend was an alien. I could be very helpful in planning for the societal transition if and when that day will come. If an alien invasion ever happens, at first people will panic and the government will need leaders who already have an in-depth understanding of the problem.

Working with the aliens, rather than fighting them, could be very profitable for the human race and planet Earth. Their advanced technology could be very helpful in numerous ways. My alien ex-boyfriend could become invisible. I knew when he would be in my house because he had a very loud step or the whole floor started shaking from his heavy weight. He is like 300 pounds so imagine the noise he was making.

My life is like a paranormal thriller movie, filled up with aliens, dead people and fairies at once. I just simply love it; because even if I try and try, I cannot stop this from happening to me. I really didn't want aliens or trouble in my life anymore. I started to dance, drink, and smoke because I wanted to forget about all this alien psychic crap. But it is still here with me and it won't stop. I really cannot do anything about it.

I got my degree and I cannot find a job. I have been dancing for two years now, and cannot handle this life any more. I pray to Lord Jesus every day now to help me find a good job so that I can stop dancing but it's not easy with this economy now. I have been looking for a job for three months now and I have only gotten two good interviews. One was to be a project manager and second to work as a paralegal.

My astrologer told me about how hard it is to have a psychic prediction for yourself—it's like a doctor operating on himself, it doesn't work. I really don't want to know my future anymore. This is my broken heart speaking because I desired someone who is not available. I truly thought that Hazy was the man who I could be happy with forever and after. But he is so self-absorbed and only cares about his money and his penis. I didn't feel that he really loved me.

A year before I met Hazy my astrologer told me that my next

relationship would be my last. That it would be the one relationship that I have been waiting for my whole life. My astrologer also told me that this guy will have to go thru his personal hell to learn more about himself, how to be honest and talk our lives together. What's more, he told me that we could even break up for some time because my partner would be self-absorbed with his own problems that this would make me feel like he didn't love me. Apparently, when his problems would end, I will see how much he really loves me.

I feel like this prediction is exactly what is happening right now with Hazy and me. He's only thinking about his court case and money problems, not thinking about me. Also I think that he wasn't honest with me. He was constantly testing me whether I loved him or his money. For my birthday he asked me to exchange with him $50 cash for $100 food stamps, so he would then use this cash to buy me a gift. He had lost his job two months before my birthday and was relying on his mother for financial support at that time. I was making good money so I had started paying for our dinners and lunches together. Anyway, I gave him that stupid $50 cash. He gave me $100 in food stamps, what was a good deal. For my birthday, all he gave me was a shawl that I think cost him only $10 at Wal-Mart. He had always bought me flowers in the past, so I asked him where my birthday flowers were. And he said to me "you will eat your flowers tonight on dinner, since I don't have enough money right now." I got so upset because I thought he should have saved up at least $100 or $200 to get me something really nice. I was always so generous to him, like two weeks before that I took him to very nice restaurant and spend $200 on dinner. I am a single mother and it's a lot of money for me because I could spend this money on my son not on the guy who doesn't care for me like I did care for him.

I told him this and he said to me, "You see your reaction to this right now, but what if I had $1 million in my bank account, would you react the same way?"

"What are you talking about?" I asked. But he never explained this to me, got so upset even more.

"You see, you see, it's not the same reaction. You should have the same reaction on both situations. First you will want to half of my money and then you will want my entire mother's money. Is Cooper paying you money to spy on me so he can win the court case?"

I was so hurt by his words. I could not believe that he thinks so low of me. In one way I understand him because his mother's ex-husband supposedly stole $ 5 million from her. I told him many times before when he asked me, that I would sign a prenuptial agreement. But he kept getting upset again and again and saying like this "oh you want start marriage without trust?" So it looks like I could not make him happy ether way because he just didn't know what he wanted in the first place. I wouldn't be able to trust people if I had had his experiences too, but not everybody is like this.

Chapter 4
Sexual confusion

I never really understood why people are so obsessed with sex. I had lived without sex for almost 4 years in my 20's when I had thought that I wanted to be an Indian nun. I only started to understand the draw of sex when I started to read books on Tantra and rise of Kundalini. Then I started to have sex for spiritual reasons not just for fun. This confusion is understandable; honestly I grow up in a strict catholic country where sex is thought to be just for reproduction. Any other type of sex or masturbation, for fun is considered a bad and shameful thing.

When I started study Tantra I think I finally understood the meaning of relationships. To become sexually fulfilled you need a tantric lover. You can make yourself tantric lover, if you practice Tantra. Hazy for sure is a tantric lover; he can come like 7 times in one night and have sex for hours if he wants to. It is so unfair that a man can come every single time he has sex while a woman needs to learn her body at first. Some women don't come at all. Guys use women for sex all the time. They are interested in their own gratification and most of the time they don't care if the woman had an orgasm or not.

At OZ I listen to all the different stories from married guys. So this guy tells me about wife divorcing his friend after 20 years of marriage with two kids for another woman. The husband was devastated that she left him for a women, but his friend told me that he never eaten her pussy for these 20 years. So when she met this women and she gave her so much pleasure the wife just turned gay. Hey if that was me I would have dumped him a long time ago.

Hazy was the same way, I was dating him for 9 months and I sucked his penis and drank his juice every single time we had sex because I loved him and wanted to make him happy, but he only kissed my pussy 5 times. I told him let's do 69 more often, he said yes, but he never did. So again we women have to give and give but not take pleasure. Why? I refuse to give and give only. I want my pleasure too. And I don't want to feel guilty about it afterwards either. Sex is good and not bad. God created our body with the capacity to enjoy ourselves with sex, so this is what we should do! Like a man once said to me, "Man was created first and his ways were basic and

41

simple. Woman was created second so she was an improvement and she was light and airy."

You must admit, and I think many people will agree, that women bodies are the most beautiful creation of God. Women's bodies are complex. They hold the secret of creation and the secret of pleasure. The bodies of men are more basic and direct, that is why they can have orgasm every time they have sex. Tantra teaches about cosmic orgasms which can last like 20-30 minutes. A tantric orgasm fills the whole body and is not limited only to the genital area. It took me 38 years to learn this and to find the right sexual partner. First time I ever experienced an orgasm like this I wasn't even having sex. I know that sounds strange, go figure, but I did. I was at this spiritual seminar about reaching your highest potential in relationships with a speaker from New Zealand. Around 30 people we were laying down on the floor with their strait spine and their eyes closed. The speaker used his voice to guide us through the paths to sexual purity. After 5-10 minutes, he started to touch everybody with one finger on their belly button, a touch which symbolized an opening and release. When he touched me, I felt a hot, energy wash thru my whole body. It was so hot that I could not stand this at first but then it turned to waves of orgasmic feeling that lasted for the next 20 minutes. I was in total bliss from my toes to my head. I didn't want it to stop at all.

Sex with Hazy introduced me to this cosmic orgasm with a partner. Our first time, I was screaming so loud, I felt absolutely no shame expressing my body's joy. I was so loud, the neighbors probably heard! Although Hazy first introduced this organism to me, he then said that I shouldn't be so loud. Once he said this, I started feel shame again and it stopped my orgasm during our sex later on that day.

Yes, I think women have trouble experiencing an orgasm because we feel shame in the pleasure of it. Our whole society says sex is bad, feel shame, and this message blocks our brain from cosmic pleasure. But screaming can be a release, a way past that shame. Like my belly button, my cosmic orgasmic spirit was released. Despite my noise, Hazy still had his orgasm. So whenever you feel like screaming from pleasure, please do and don't let anybody make you feel ashamed about this.

I wasn't a screamer before I met Hazy. I was starting my new life, so I stopped worrying about what he would think of me and focused on my pleasure. I remember, he said to me "Baby we can make porn movies together when we make love like this." He was my first sexual partner where I could let go of my all fears of judgment. I just wanted to have finally great sex. I guess my sexual frustration is how I could go from being a nun to a stripper. I even didn't know that I was sexually frustrated until I started dancing. My guilt over experiencing pleasure was buried so deep that I didn't care too much about my sexual life. Yes, I did masturbate all the time, but I just kind of gave up on guys to give me orgasms since they weren't so good and didn't care much at the first place. I don't like one night stands and so I wasn't having much sex. Altogether they are not worth it.

But it takes a tantric lover to give you tantric orgasms. A tantric lover is the one who likes to have sex all the time and for long periods. Some people, those with lots of shame, might call this man a sex-addict. If a sex addict, tantric lover finds a right woman he might be able to change his values and focus on one woman. What am I saying . . . guys don't change, we all know that. They may pretend they do, but I read a study that found only about 12-15% of any addicts is able to change their behavior. Men or women, this slim chance at change is unfortunate.

I am so depressed and still frustrated. I don't want to be with anybody when I get like this. I don't know where all my psychic abilities are and why they are not helping me like they always have in the past. I think that Saturn brings delays and perhaps this has caused me to be so down. I read in my horoscope, that the two year passing of Saturn through Aries is over now, so perhaps good things will arrive here any moment now. A happy ending should be all good now, but I know that is not even funny to believe in astrology any more. I can reject these stars and predictions, and hide from what is happening but then it hits me right in the face, like a slap on the cheek. Reality always brings the right outcome soon or later.

Ok, I have a Pollack joke for you: Do you know why almost all

Pollack's are alcoholics? Because they suck vodka from their mother's nipples. I love this joke! Maybe because I made it up all by myself.

Hazy is not good at taking a real joke, I think he is too self-centered for that. When somebody calls him an N-word, he punches them. Personally I don't believe in violence like this. People call me a stupid Pollack all the time, but I learned to turned this around and joke about this. Life is too short, and if you cannot take a joke about yourself and don't have a real sense of humor, you just might get sick.

I feel like brainless, when a woman, especially when a very sexy woman, wants me sexually. She can make me feel so confused and horny. I have liked men my whole life but now so many women especially here in USA want to hook up with me. It's different when my good girl-friend gets drunk and tells me that I am so cute and delicious, and want to make out with me for fun. But it's different, when this comes from a hot strange woman. If girls will keep hitting on me so many times, that makes me think that maybe I should give it a try. I told myself when I will turn 40, which is year and a half from now, if I haven't found true love with a man then I will try to be a lesbian. Or else I will try to marry old millionaire which are plenty here in Florida. I don't know, will see later.

I want to believe that love will find me for now and forever more. I know my life's plan, but this is not it. I'm a psychic, exotic dancer, with a BS in criminology and psychology, who cannot find a real job. What a Pollack. I need to keep this light and funny though, because sometimes all we can do in life is laugh at ourselves.

No matter what, being serious is boring. As a 100% Aries pure woman, I can't handle being bored at all. For my 30th birthday I tried skydiving. Wow! That was really awesome. It was a tandem jump with the instructor strapped to my back. Another guy, jumped with us and video tapped my free fall. The plane had no doors, so when I was standing on the edge of plane and looked down, before I jumped, I thought that I might pass out from fear. I thought "why the hell I am doing this to myself?" But at the same moment the guy strapped to me pushed us and we started our free fall. The air pressure was so strong that I couldn't breathe. It was a nightmare for whole one minute. But after the parachute opened up, it was pure bliss for the next eight minutes. When we landed I was ready to do it again. So when I turn 40, if my prince charming still has not found me I will turn gay and bisexual. Marry millionaire and do sky diving again.

What a change, can bring a new chance for love again. I am tired with guys who act like a pussy so I might as well try real pussy. Oh . . . I hear from men all the time that I am too strong, too scary, too independent, or to weird. Also I don't want the verbal and physical abuse that I put up with during my relationship with my shape-shifting alien boyfriend. Dating an abusive alien can really make you lose faith in men. So yes, becoming a lesbian is probably my new life direction. Anyways, girls are less aggressive and more fun. They want me so bad and I want to have fun and be wanted. My only one problem is that I like warm and juicy penises, not the plastic ones. But no worries yet, I will see how it works after my 40th birthday.

Anyway, I met many women who were physically abused by their husbands and they had to divorce them. But after such a terrible experience women they just don't want a man anymore. Sounds like a good reason to turn gay. I have two lesbian girlfriends who work at OZ and they still had boyfriends. Only after so many disappointing relationships did they finally turn gay. For some women, it's a conscious choice. Those lesbian exotic dancers they actually go back and forward because one of these girls, after 3 years of being lesbian, she just got a boyfriend . . . What a change!

Lesbians they can be very sexy. One woman that I met at OZ who became a lesbian when she was just 14 years old. It was illegal for her to have sex with boys at that age, she got frustrated, so instead of keeping it in, she tried sex with girls and liked it.

This is totally natural, I think. I did really my best in this last relationship with Hazy. I swallowed his juice every time we had sex, we have sex in my booty a lot, I cooked for him and I cleaned his house. I even was willing to try going to a swing house. And still he dumped me because I supposedly complained too much about his mother not like me.

He was the one who was always talking about getting married. I gave him everything I could, but it still was not good enough. I really don't know what guys want these days. Yes, sadly I still, love Hazy very much. And yes, I have to admit I was upset with his mom, but I did like her. She is a very talented woman, but despite this, she is very controlling.

Hazy's mother wrote a play about polish stripper with green eyes and a red nose. This is me 100%. She invited about 60 people to a small theatre to see the actors do the play. I was invited of course, but I didn't have a clue till the play was played that it was all about me. Her joke was that everybody knew the play was about me, so they all had so much fun on my expense. She totally humiliated me. Even one of her friends came up to me and Hazy and asked him "Did you know about this? Did you have anything to do with it?"

But of course Hazy said no, I learned that he was telling her everything that I was telling him about my life. I felt like she robbed me of my life. I know I can be very inspirational to people. But for God sake, I want to write about my own life, not have her steal my stories and embarrass me on purpose in front of all her friends. But my life is the one that is interesting, the one that people want to hear about. So Charlotte mama, I am sorry, I forgive you. I send you golden light. I love you.

I was so in love with Hazy, I had lost hope in relationships before, Hazy gave me light and hope for nine months and now he is gone. Now I feel anger and pain again.

I need to try being gay real soon. I am so tired of working at night, too much alcohol, long nights. I don't know but somehow I can see this must have been written in the stars. All because my name Kamilah. Kamilah was the high priestess of the Goddess Isis, the Mother God, Queen of Heaven. As her high priestess, Kamilah performed rituals of praying, and dancing. Her dancing was similar to the exotic stripping that is done now. Kamilah also means the perfect one in Egyptian. My whole life was impact by this name. It's weird but when I think of Isis I think of Charlotte, Hazy's mother too. When I was 16, I started dancing in the first post-communist music hall in Poland called Metro. I was in the front line of the top modern dancers in the whole country. We were about to go to NYC to dance on Broadway when my beloved but narrow minded mom wouldn't let me go. At that time I was very shy and didn't know how to stand up for myself. I was scared because she said she would go to police and take me to jail if I didn't listen to her. Even though the communist regime was over the laws hadn't changed so quickly and she had total authority over me until I was 18.

Growing up in a communist regime, you learned that everybody else is right but never you. I was too scared to fight her back. The anger and disappointment grew so strong in me, that when I turned 18 I was ready to rebel and fight. I drop out of high school, ran away from home to work as a Go-Go Dancer in Berlin Germany. I started to make four times the money my mother did back in Poland. Still today, it's so hard for me to forget her for not allowing me to go to New York City. I do love her and respect her but the anger and pain never left me! But my destiny brought me here to the United States anyway. So I guess all it was fate something bigger than these little decisions. Some people, born in America, don't even know what a wonderful chance they have just because they are born here.

I guess the Catholic priest was right to not want to give me names Kamilah and Maria Magdalena. I mean what a loaded fate was written on those names. He knew somehow that their meanings would impact my life tremendously. Kamilah, the priestess of magic and Maria Magdalena, the prostitute.

I remember the priest said to me at my confirmation, "You know there is no saint Kamila in the Catholic Church, so you better make good choices in your life. And then you'll have a chance to become a Saint"

I was like ha-ha, what are you talking about dude? Me? A saint, which was rather a crazy idea but the spirit was in me and I did become a Hindu nun for 4 years. I am spiritual not just in the Catholic faith that I was born into, but spirit is shared among many different beliefs and religions. Still . . . . I hope they all count in the end.

My tattoo reminds me of the choice I made about my sexuality—to never forget that controlled sex is the way also to nirvana. Many people believe that Egyptian gods were in fact aliens living among us. I came to the same conclusion.

My life unconditional love rule is that love must be given with a free heart. Real love doesn't come from magic or voodoo. Last night I had this sexual dream with Hazy and this other couple. The woman started to suck her man's penis in front of us and then Hazy opened his pants and pulled out his penis. In the dream I didn't like that at all and got really upset at him. That was odd to me, when I woke up because I talk and think about swing sex all the time lately.

About 2 years ago, I did try being a lesbian. She had the name Nefertiti, the same name as an Egyptian goddess. We had sex on my couch and in my guest bedroom too. It was awesome. I wasn't ready at the time for anything other than experimenting sex with a woman. Too bad I deleted her number. I wish I could meet her again.

Chapter 5
Mind freak of mine

On Discovery Channel they have TV shows that talk a lot about aliens and how they theoretically created the human race from mixing their alien DNA with chimpanzees. By having sex and children with us, the aliens want to help us humans reach our true potential. The aliens love us, and their creation, they want to keep improving us with more alien DNA. They are ready to come down again and live among humans, but this time they will stay on Earth for good. Their planet is dying. But our planet is in trouble too so we need them; we need their technology to save us from the same outcome. We cannot continue to explore the natural resources of our planet and pollute the Earth so much like we do right now. I feel like Queen Isis wants me to be her highest priestess again. I hear the calling. Yes, I am not afraid anymore. I am fearless leader now. I would like to see her again. I would like to see the alien Queen and pray and dance for her.

The American Navy they have Isis golden wings as their logo. Some people think that the aliens live in bases deep under the water. I would like to be hired by the Navy for that reason and for communication with dolphins and the aliens. The alien bases are classified information and the government doesn't let you talk about it. I met this retired astronaut at work one time and of course I have to ask him if he saw any aliens in space. He didn't want to admit at first but later yes he told me he saw enormous spaceships passing very slowly like they wanted to be seen.

Peter's father worked for 10 years here in America in NYC at the World Bank. Many of the aliens shape shifters are important politicians and celebrities. Apparently they want to live here because they like beer and human girls.

Shambhala Kingdom in the Himalayas is a secret mythical Buddhist Kingdom. Shambhala is believed to be a society where all the inhabitants are enlightened. It is commonly understood to be a place of peace, tranquility, and happiness. Spiritual guards, protect the mysterious door that leads to Shambhala. After reading this book about Shambhala, I had dream with a woman with bright white skin, no hair, and brilliant eyes. She telepathically said to me, "Tuesday at 10am I will send you a message from the Shambhala Kingdom." I then woke up and I could not forget her face, she was so beautiful. When Tuesday came I didn't know what to do, so I started to meditate at home. While meditating, I saw myself and two friends from a distance. Above us was this man levitating. He was a guardian of the Shambhala Kingdom and he spoke to me, "The door to the Kingdom can be open anytime you want to enter, but it will not open for your friends. They cannot see or hear me, but you can do it anytime if you work to control your energy." I would love to enter that Kingdom right now if it was possible please.

Isis has these beautiful wings, like the wings of an angel intertwined with a snake. At Home Depot, one time, this guy he stands right next to me, he had a baseball hat with those Isis's wings and snake between. He said looking into my eyes "We want to cooperate." I was so shocked. I said nothing and just walked anyway. He was an alien, I know for sure. I feel like alien males, they want to talk to me. I know this is irrational, so I pretend like nothing just happened.

Krakow is the best place in Poland to go to. It was the first capitol of Poland. They say the last dragon was killed at the Wawel Castle right in downtown. The Hindu religion believes that is where Lord Siva laid one of the holy seven stones. The God Siva threw out seven stones into the world. Where they landed became great centers of energy that radiates out from these points. This is like the Seven Chakras in the human body. The Wawel Chakra is the Heart Charka of planet Earth. I would like to go to see other planets, travel on a trip with Lord Siva. Ha-ha. Hindu people on special occasions pray to the Heart Chakra. They bring flowers and do pujas there sometimes, not too often though.

Yes, I remember those days form 11 years ago. Meditating 4 hours a day, fasting for weeks and not talking, of course yoga nonstop. It was fun, fun, fun . . . . I miss those days sometimes, but my destiny was to have a child and come down from my life as a Hindu nun to my life as a mother filled with attachment. I have my son now and I would never change that for anything. Before that I didn't need much. I was so easily able to reach the level of detachment from the pain and pleasure of this world. Now, I am crying over a broken heart

and the lack of sex in my life. Before I was Hindu nun devoted
to find enlightenment. Now I am a exotic dancer. What a trip,
but they say there are many different ways to enlightenment.

Yes, back in Poland I had my own business on the sea side
selling swims suits. My company was called Jointex. Yes, I did
smoke pot earlier in my life, this is something that I have
returned to right now, I smoke pot one week and the next week
I don't smoke it. It works for me. I know I have very strong will,
I think that comes from being a Hindu nun with ten years of
meditation. I don't even talk about my spiritual past anymore
to people who I meet now. They just don't believe me that I
could have lived that life. I don't care what they think of me, I
don't need them to believe in me. As long I believe in myself I
am perfectly fine. I totally understand this is crazy believing in
all that alien agenda and shape shifters and all other stories
of my life. But are crazy people aware of their craziness in the
first place? I really try to avoid my whole life, this so called
psychic powers, but is still happening to me regardless even if I
drink and smoke to pollute my body. This self-medicating, just
makes it happen a little less frequently.

I saw Hazy today walking with two women one on each side,
like some kind of macho parade or something. I stopped; I
could not face him like this. Thank God he didn't look to my
side because I was like 10 feet away only. What I would say?
"Hey baby I still love you and miss you like crazy."

No, never. I will not run after a penis who doesn't want me
anymore. If he would love me and wanted me, he would have
come back to me a long time ago. It's probably like I said
before, that white voodoo he put on me is still working. He
messed up this relationship because of his continued testing of
me. That was too much stress, constantly trying to prove myself
to him. I really don't like to be tested like some kind of lab rat.
Nobody would like that.

So I have this most irrational feeling that Hazy is not only
taping my cell phone, but also using my laptop camera and my
cable box to watch me while I am at home. I know that he has
this surveillance program set up at his mom and grandparents
apartments. I think he is so scared for my and his life because
of this Cooper monster who threatens us. OMG, so he loves me

that much? Or am I just tripping again? Some people at OZ told me about a sex video with me and him is now online. I know Hazy and I had sex all the time in front of his computer. I remember last year he asked me about recording what happens around his house, put the video on YouTube to get more attention for his court case. I told him don't put any video of me online because I don't like it. I never wanted to be a porn star, being a dancer is hard enough.

He said "What if we get famous?"

"I don't want to be famous, not like this anyway. I will sue you if you do that to me."

"What about getting rich than?" He asked me.

"Rich is ok."

"Then all is ok." And he laughed.

Funny because my astrologer, who is the sweetest gay guy ever, told me like 10 years ago that I might get famous, but I might not want all the attention. Apparently I have been famous in my past life and I know how hard it is to handle the public pressure and constant judgment. Well, I like attention for sure, but if the people are watching me online and I don't even know about it, what can I do about it? This is crazy and it's a crime. But if he loves me that much, why he is not here? And if I love him that much, I shouldn't have a problem with his posting our sex tape online, right? Why do American guys do wild stuff like this? But then do this behind my back without telling me directly? I have to find out by hearing strange comments from people I don't even know.

In new age spirituality they say that God sends his message though everything and everybody. I want to know, not be kept in the dark. I know Hazy wants me, he wants me bad. I want him the same way. He is so mucho. I love it, this macho-ness but not always. I don't like guys who act like puppets. But he is so mucho to me while he is a puppet for his mom. I want a man who can tell me what to do when he is right and I want to tell him what to do when I am right. Like equals. We might think differently as a man and woman, but we want the same things in the end. We want peace, happiness, freedom and trust.

This is power struggle between the sexes. I don't understand why. Women hold the secret of life and creation. I am responsible for this, not men. Men need to understand that women don't want to fight; we just want to be listened to and cared for. A penis is not superior to a pussy. The two need each other. Yes we need your sperm and your juicy penises. Relationships between man and woman should be protected.

I am sorry to be so direct about these power struggles between the sexes. I just talk aggressive if I feel strongly about something. I remember during middle school and high school I could always talk out everybody out of a fight, I was the peacemaker and the protector to others when they were bullied. Somehow I was very convincing so everybody listened to me. I guess that comes from being Chinese Tiger, this makes me a big protector, even when I was 15 years old.

Hazy, what am I supposed to do? I miss him; sure I still love him too. This is like way too crazy to keep going on. But since I am not too sane myself, I tend to attract other crazy people like me. Besides, a psychology study proved that being in love is like being crazy. Passionate love and cocaine high produce the same reactions in our brain. Our brain produce too much of endorphins and (PEA) phenylethylamine when we are in love that information's are unable to travel from one brain cell to another as fast as before. In fact passionate love should be called temporary insanity. We don't think as clearly as we usually do, when we are in love. Instead our brain works slower.

So Hazy went crazy because he is still madly in love with me. Well, that's great because I am still madly in love with him too. Or I imagine stuff in my head because, I am madly still in love and I have so called temporary insanity. Whichever . . . you prefer. In point of fact, both situations lead to my craziness regardless. On the other hand this whole book is like one big proof to the whole world that I am not like super crazy. I mean like mentally ill or something. For example, in 1954, American psychiatrists were prescribing some pills for poor gay guys because they believed being gay could be cured. When you look at them now, you would say that psychiatrist were crazy. So looking to the future, I could be considering totally normal before I die. Back in the 1920s here in America, husbands had a right to put their wives into psychiatric—hospitals. No documentation of mental sickness was necessary. That is why I will fight my fight to say what I want to say. I know in the future, I will be proven true and not considered crazy. Time will show sooner or later what is normal and what is not normal. Anyhow, so called "normal" is redefined every decade or so, for last 100 years or even less, since human kind speeds up evolution in every possible direction. So entirely thinkable, I will be completely normal in 10 years from now or even fewer. My ex-shape shifting boyfriend told me that alien DNA will be discovered soon in our life time.

In four days, I am going to do a fire walk here in Saint Petersburg Florida. I am so excited I will be walking on hot burning wood at 900 Fahrenheit temperature. I know this sound wild, but I have done this once before back in Europe. It was the greatest experience ever. It was like walking on very hot sand on the beach. Little bit burning but no pain at all. I refuse to live in fear because only you should be fearful of fear itself. Every new age person knows that. Fear is an opposite emotion to love. Choose love above fear because love is all there is. I really hope I will feel something new this time when I walk on the fire. I really would like to feel what it is like to be on fire and I want the fire to burn all my fears away.

I would also like to feel as-one with dolphins. I would like to feel as-one with the aliens. I would like to feel as-one with everything. You see, for a new age person like myself this is completely normal. But for most so called "normal" people I am freak and I am truly aware of it. Even people at work who I have known for two years now they don't have a single clue as to who I really am. For them I am just exotic dancer who happened to have some brain cells left and went to grad school for two semesters in Biostatistics. Which, I actually did. I went to grad school.

So what can I do about it? Hide my whole life? I am 38 years old. I cannot hide anymore. The crazy night life at OZ has to come to end soon because I drink way too much there. I went to doctor today because my chest pain and she said it's because of stress . . . I have high blood pressure too. I know that is because I drink too much alcohol. I want to be pure again but maybe not to the extreme purity like I was before with no sex, no alcohol, no meat, no anything. Just meditation and yoga. Oh well, definitely I need to stop drinking liquor. Maybe I just drink beer and wine now. Funny, because before I started dancing I almost never drank liquor at all. Now I become true Polak and all I drink is vodka.

This is little scary for me, for I worry that if I stop polluting myself then all the visions will start again. I know if I start meditating again and do lots of yoga my third eye will work again. I know that many people would consider these visions a blessing, but they don't know how hard it is to handle all this extra information.

I like telepathy because I experience it all the time. Particularly with people I love, like family and close friends. Today for example. I was thinking that I truly wanted to lose 15 pounds to come back to my perfect weight and be a size 4 again. I have so many clothes in my closet that are size 4. I am now size 6. I thought to myself that I should drink more water not juice because juice has too many calories. Ha-ha. The fruit juice, not the other juice.

Not even 10 minutes later my beloved son Amadeus came up to me and asked me "Mommy, do you think I am skinny?"

"Yes, son you are very skinny. Funny you said that."

"You want to drink more water to be skinnier, right?" He said. I smiled, at how we all experience little unintentional telepathic moments like this. But imagine if we could do that all the time. We would be able to know the true intentions of everybody. I think that will be awesome because it will save us so much drama.

Since I don't have sex now, I can start to focus on exercising my pelvic muscle that is responsible for cosmic orgasms. The muscle that you contract when you hold a pee. We theoretically, have to come up to 100 contractions in one setting to make the muscle stronger. That is according to Tantra philosophy. This is exercise for both women and men.

Men can strengthen this muscle to hold their erection longer during intercourse. Now I can do easy 100 contractions in one set, but when I started practicing I only could do like 25 repetitions. The normal orgasm can stand only up to 10 contractions of that muscle. If you exercise this muscle like I did, the contractions can be a long time apart so the orgasm can last longer than 10 seconds. You can have orgasm last for like 10-20 minutes. I remember when we had sex, Hazy asked me sometimes contract that muscle while he was inside me because it feels good on his penis like a massage.

I met this lady at my sons pre-kindergarten. Her son was the only boy essentially taller than Amadeus, in the same age group. I asked her how tall his father is. She told me that both her sons, 5 and 3 years old are from a sperm bank and she had no clue about how tall their father was. She was lesbian living with her girlfriend. Bizarre. I thought you were able to choose if you want a tall sperm donor or not. We started talking about my idea to trying being a lesbian. She told me, she experienced even more drama in her relationships with women than with men, because women tend to be more emotional. Well, I guess I will be bisexual then. I will swing in both ways, whoever will give me more pleasure.

I watched Oprah TV the other night and there was a program about swinger couples in America. People who are already swingers were giving advice to new comers. They suggested that couples should just go there and play between each other at first because you really don't know how you will react to swinging the first time. I want to experiment sexually but I am like scared if I have sex with random guy or girl without feelings it's not going to be as good as when you are actually in love.

So instead I watch porn all the time. I started watching porn 3 years ago only. That's funny how people change. Look at me I came from Hindu nun to an exotic dancer porn watcher.

America is the best country in the whole world because shape shifter-aliens are so powerful here. Look at the Hollywood, there must be tons of them there because most of the movies are about aliens now. It's like they are sending a message for the public to prepare for the aliens to come out real soon.

Chapter 5
Diamond child

*T*he alien Queen has pale white skin with eyes that are a mix of blue, green, purple, and black. She has eyes like a peacock's feather. The aliens come from a very cold planet that is basically dead. There are other planets like earth that they could move to, but they like ours best. Earth is the most advanced technologically and humans already share an evolutionary history with the aliens. Plus many of us think they are Gods. What's not to like about that?

They would like to advance our technology, because essentially they want to free us from faulty notions about ourselves and about them. Most of them they don't want to take human body form because they find it restrictive. Some of the aliens are much bigger and taller than humans and of course they have bigger brains too. This can be awkward and uncomfortable to squish together when they shape shift into human form.

I have seen a door in my dreams twice now. The first time was when Peter told me to move to St. Petersburg Florida. In the dream we were running fast to huge door like a gate, but when we got there it wouldn't open. Yesterday, I had a dream where I saw door opening to reveal a mirror of energy and the beautiful alien Queen. I wasn't afraid, so I talked to the alien Queen. She told me that she rather prefers to stay in her natural form.

Scientologists have also been tracking me for last nine years. I am surprised I didn't get a letter from them yet in my new place. Yes, they always try to contact me when I change addresses. They in fact, visited my best friend here Nene in her house yesterday. Five Scientologists told her to take care of her teeth and not kill anybody. Wow, what a spooky message, but makes sense. Clean healthy teeth are important. Maybe I should accept their invitation after nine years and visit their church. Of course I would like to see Tom Cruise and John Travolta if they would be there for a service. Since I am not scared of aliens I shouldn't be scared of scientology. That should be interesting to hear, what essentially they have to say about it. But I don't want to pay for all that knowledge because they are expensive with their required donations. Or so I was told.

If I was meant to, and I certainly hope so, to talk to aliens as the representative for humanity, then I need my strong man like Hazy standing side by side with me in my life. Some people may want to become more alien and this is possible with alien DNA injections.

I saw a black butterfly while I was watching TV. He flew next to my chair and then disappeared. I tried to find him but I could not see him anywhere. I need my guardian angels to take care of me. I really like some help right now please. Beloved archangel Chamuel help me to heal my spiritual soul mate relationship please. I want my Hazy back.

I walked on fire last Saturday, three times. I walked once for myself, once for Hazy, and once for our relationship. I should have walked more for my mom and his mom, but I burned my toes a little bit. I sure do hope the fire burned away all my fears. I refuse to live in fear; I want to live in love. Why Hazy baby is not coming back, I don't understand.

I wish I could have more time to talk to that alien Queen from my dream. I would tell her then, when they take over the world, there has to be no killing this time. There is no need for a death fight over the Earth. Mass killing would be pointless because they want to help us! The aliens already have a big base underwater in Bermudas and there are many other deep underwater bases spread out throughout the world. I have no idea how they are planning their takeover. Undoubtedly, it must be in a good way, since they don't want to kill us because they live here with us already.

I go back and forth feeling like I'm on the top of the world and then I crash and feel so down. Life is like an ocean, constant waves of pleasure and pain. Spiritual people say that all sickness starts in your mind. So it's like a proof of the theory of psychosomatic disorders in which the physical symptoms are caused by mental projections.

So if illness can be a psychosomatic and only show when you get upset, it totally proves the power of mind over matter.

Why I go from extreme behavior like this in my life? From being Hindu nun to being an exotic dancer? Like from saint to sinner. What is next? I really hope I will find my golden way of living, the middle path. I don't want to be extreme any more. I have had enough of excitement, and negative thinking patterns. Bitter words left unspoken while a positive affirmation to change can code your brain like a new program in the computer. I will think and speak only words of peace I am in love with my life. It is sad because I wanted to have all this wild sex and now I wonder whether I can still have it.

So if Jesus was an alien according to scientology, they have a power to heal mankind from all these sicknesses. They sound so good, so why is the government covering up the alien agenda? We need their healing and their technology. We should be in reality, happy for their coming back.

Last night I had a dream about my sister who lives in Norway now, about her giving a birth to her son, Alexander. I called my other sister Agnes in the morning and she confirmed the news of the birth of my new nephew. This is magnificent. I should take more naps. Maybe I will have a dream that I really want to see, like the lottery winning numbers.

Last night at work I met this nice guy. We were talking about poetry and he showed my some of his short poems. After a bit though he freaked me out little bit when he said "Watch TV tomorrow, something is going to happened about the stock market because it has been too steady for too long now."

I didn't pay too much attention to what he said to me that night, but first thing the next morning I turned TV on and there it was—the Stock Market was the highest level since 2008 because they found some more oil in the Gulf of Mexico. I have an odd feeling that he was shape shifter.

I had a dream with Hazy; we were in Poland at my grandma's house eating ice-cream. My grandma died last year, so I don't understand this dream. Maybe my grandma wanted to show me that she accepted and liked him? I am tired of dreaming of Hazy. We broke up four months ago and I still have dreams about him. It only hurts me more. I wish I didn't have any more dreams about him. I wish that would be over so I could move on. For sure, he is with someone else already, telling her how much he loves her. All I have are my dreams and in my broken heart. I really don't know why I still want him, after the way he treated me. I should be more cold hearted, but if I try I know is not in my nature to be cold to people. I would love to have some help here. Please Lord Jesus and all the angels please help me and save me from this madness. All I wanted is to have a good job and a good husband. I didn't want million of dollars. Is so hard to find a happy normal life? Only my son, Amadeus, gives me reason to live and move forward.

All my major problems started when I met my ex-alien boyfriend Peter/Charlie. Amadeus is his son, so he is true half alien and half human. He has more alien DNA than normal people have. He is only 5 years-old now but he started talking about paranormal stuff already. Like for example he tells me what he can see with his red eyes. I tried to ignore this when he first started speaking of this and told him to not to talk about it. But he started to share all his secrets with his best friend Alex, another 5 year-old Polish-American boy. He told him about how he can see what is going on underground and high in the sky, like he can see people while they are in the plane. First time when he was talking about his red eyes Amadeus was only 3 years-old and he asked me.

"Mommy what is wrong with me? Why I have blue and red eyes but you have only blue?"

"Baby, nothing is wrong with you. You have beautiful blue-green eyes."

He can totally read my mind all the time now. He can tell me sometimes exactly what I was just thinking about. Fifteen years ago, when I was new age freak I used to pray for a Diamond child. So here we go again, be careful of what you wish for. Maybe that is why Peter/Charlie picked me up in Geneva as a mother for his future baby boy.

One day Amadeus he was literally talking to his dad like he was standing right in front of him but invisible to me. Amadeus even had to look up, when he was listening because his dad is so very tall. Amadeus was nodding his head for yes and no in response to his dad's questions. Amadeus then looked at me to see my reaction. I love my son so much; he is my light, my sun, and my moon. Funny because Amadeus always tells me that I am his moon and he is my sun. So cute.

I just simply cannot handle this by myself anymore. It's too heavy. I wish I was normal and none of this happened to me. All I can do is my best try for the crazy ride now and in the future to protect my beloved son. I know I am not the only one with a child like this one. There are many more, I can feel that too somehow. I cannot be the only mother with a half alien child. Before, the aliens had to abduct the half alien babies because they didn't know yet how they would behave. The Government also wanted to cover up everything about aliens. Now, because they know how half alien and half human children grow up to be more understanding, the aliens don't have to abduct the children anymore. It is better when children grow up with their natural mothers. Also the public is becoming more accepting to aliens now.

I know I sound like I might be an expert about aliens but I am just telling my everyday life experience. I wish I could have more information now directly from aliens. I would most like to hear from alien females not just from male's aliens. Father of my son, my ex-alien boyfriend told me many times, about how he tried to be with me in our past lives. I didn't want to be with him then, but somehow this lifetime I change my mind. Well, I could only imagine how hard it is to remember your past lives. I know many spiritual people say that it might be overwhelming to know about your past lives and this knowledge might stop you from learning the lesson in this lifetime. Therefore is hidden in our brain so we won't have to remember. No wonder why we use only 15% of our brain.

My son, I really worry about him. How can I protect him more? I want him to be better man than his father. Peter/Charlie himself has told me to tell this to Amadeus "I want you to be better man than your father" Amadeus asked me today "Where is your boyfriend Hazy? He is still your boyfriend right Mommy?" My little boy 5 years-old and already so smart. Amadeus pointed at the clock on the wall that Hazy had given to me.

"You see mommy, this is time right? We have to wait, we cannot change it. And nothing is weird."

Amadeus knows that we have to hide our psychic abilities a little bit longer. Amadeus has super strong hearing abilities. He can hear my thoughts. They reach him like radio waves. He doesn't gave me too much hard time with what he knows, he is sweet little boy. Of course he is spoiled brat as any normal American child, crying maybe too much to get his way. Otherwise, he is pure unconditional love and joy for all the times. I really wish that Amadeus turns out to be a better man than his father. His father could be very annoying and drank way too much. He could become very aggressive and always blamed me for everything. He blamed me for the sacrifices he made in his career. Instead of continuing being a politician, he has chosen to play the guitar on the corner in downtown St. Petersburg Florida and lives of a government disability check.

It is good that he tries to be in Amadeus's life, but he is a depressed alcoholic and needs help. I have tried to help him so many times but his deep alcoholism and his longing for his politician carrier in Switzerland is so big, that he should go back there and forget about me and Amadeus, because his being here in this state of mind is no good for any of us. Although Amadeus loves him very much. Hopefully the aliens will reveal themselves soon and this will help my family.

I really hope the aliens will not take Amadeus from me, because Peter/Charlie once said to me, "half alien children only need mothers until they are 5 or 6 years-old, after that they don't need parents."

He has tried to intimidate me many times, saying that when Amadeus turns 5, he would take him away from me. I would fight for my son and would absolutely never let this happen. So I pray to Jesus to help me and my son stay together. Anyway, Amadeus told me that he loves us both the same but he wants to live with me. So far I can sleep in peace. Amadeus also told me that he wants to live with me when he goes to college. Although, I got this frightening dream that Amadeus was selected to a very prestigious private school in different state but they would only let me see him on weekends. Then I woke up and I hoped this was only a bad dream. I don't want to lose my son like that. Isn't that what they believe in Scientology? Those 6 years-old children should be separated from parents to live in a boarding school. Wow, I don't think I would ever want that. This is different when your baby is 16 year-old teenager, but at 6, he is still my real baby.

Well, I remember Peter/Charlie told me one day, which if he took me back to Switzerland and returned to his normal body as Peter that I would never complete my dream of becoming an independent successful woman. I am 38 years old; for sure I am independent, but I am far from being successful. Peter/Charlie also said that my life should be here in the USA not in Switzerland. I have to admit I miss Switzerland sometimes even more than I miss Poland. I had a great four years of my life over there with tons of good friends. Here I am always almost alone. One of my astrologers told me that I would be most happy in California or Chicago. Yes, California has perfect weather, beautiful mountains and the breathtaking ocean. Chicago has a large polish community. Where to go? Someone help me, please!

I cannot be alone forever. I am too hot for that, everybody is telling me this. Sometimes I feel like I am too picky, or I just don't want to waste my time on guys that are no good anymore. I don't know what to do with myself. No sex for now. I am tired of this negative energy, pessimism and hunger to be loved.

We all want to be in love, but why is so hard to find it? Being in love is such a great feeling, especially in the beginning. So where is my special man? The man that was promised to me. He is late, of course. The process of Saturn must be slowing him down. But this month Saturn is passing into my sign of Aries. All these dreams and visions mean nothing to me if I wait my whole life for someone who is a figment of my imagination. My whole life I have been searching for a universal spiritual truth, but I feel like I am in the same place as where I started 17 year ago. I have learned nothing.

I should be better example for my son. He is so sweet. He is telling me lately that he never wants to grow up, and wants to be 5 years old forever. Oh, I had dream couple days ago with me and Amadeus. We were in the Swiss mountains having a picnic with my very best friend Angelica and her daughter Dominica. We were all having such a relaxing time. In another dream I was flying so high in the sky and fast like a superwoman, I could dive also into the water and swim fast like a dolphin. What a trip that was, so much adrenalin and happiness. I loved it. Well, I might be little psychic after all because last night I had a dream where at work I made $200 and something. I went today to work and I made $240. This was close to the amount of money that I dreamed about last night. It's still happening against my will to see. I should just accept what was given to me. That gift of foreseen dreams . . .

I think I have a double life. One in real life, and one, in my dreams. At least both my waking life and my dreams are very exciting.

I know I can give unconditional love to many people. I know that also, more than ever in the relationship, love should be given unconditionally.

Chapter 7
Pink bubble

I was thinking about my son Amadeus. I should be more supportive of his capabilities because I don't want to stop him from developing in the future. It's very scary when he starts talking about stuff beyond my comprehension. I am also scared of what he is telling to his 5 year old friend. I love my Amadeus so much and I cannot change what he is, therefore, I have to support him no matter what.

He was behaving very badly at school. Lately, he got several red lights and he was suspended twice already in the first two months of school. So I hide all his toys and told him no TV and no computer games. Instead he sat up in his room all alone. I went to go check up on him, since he was so quiet for a while. When I walked into his room, I saw him levitating close to the ceiling. I said "Wow, Amadeus that is awesome. I want to do the same thing you do."

He started smiling and spinning around real fast.

"How do you do that son?"

"Well mommy, you can do this too. But you need to train your will power and change your belief system."

"How do you know that? You are just 5 year old boy."

"Mommy, I love the way you are, but you need to understand something about planet Earth. Earth has a lot of water. In other planets there is no water at all. Humans are made of golden light and you can do just same as me. You just don't know that yet. If you don't know that, you don't believe. If you don't believe, you cannot fly like I am right now."

"Oh yes, darn smarty pants, so outspoken, but why are you so bad behaving at school than?"

"Oh mommy, I am still only 5 years old. I want to have fun, run around and play. I don't need to be so serious yet."

"Oh my son, what am I going to do with you?"

"Mommy, don't worry I will protect you."
I think he might be right because I remember my flying night dreams. I have flown in my dreams for the past 17 years. When I can't levitate in my dreams then that is when I tend to feel depressed in my awake life. I could feel the connection.

"Amadeus please do not show this levitating to Alex or anyone, OK? You know what people don't understand and they will be afraid of."

"I know that mommy. That is why I have super mother like you who understands me and accepts me the way I am. I love you mommy. I love you forever."

"I love you my son, no matter what, and forever more. I just want to keep it safe for both of us. I cannot lose you. You are my one and only everything."

"Ok mommy, I will be good at school, I promise."

Last Monday at about 7.30 pm, somebody pounded at my door. I was scared at first. Oh dear Lord Jesus I don't want to live in fear anymore. Please angels help me have a better life. I am so tired today, too many emotions for one day. My son is a sweetheart but I am so scared for him. I feel like all these emotions drain my energy.

Last night at work, this Asian guy came up to me and asked me. I never met him before.

"Do you think I am evil?"

"What kind of question is that?" I said.

"Do you think I am evil?"

"No, not at all. I don't think you are evil. Why?" I started playing his game, "Did you do something evil?"

"Oh, you gave me hope and I love your smile. You are so sexy. I am part machine, human, and alien. The human part comes here most because I love pussy the same as everybody else does and I have no money."

"What are you talking about? You are freaking me out. I got to go now."

I had to stop him. This was not one on one psychiatric therapy in a strip club. Bye-bye. What a creep. Thank God he didn't shape shift right there in front of everybody. Although when I think about it now, that wouldn't be such a bad idea after all. It would be awesome because OZ has cameras everywhere and that would be solid proof. A shape shifter in a strip club would make front page news. Or nobody would pay any attention to it in the first place.

My sinus congestion is killing me today, headache and runny nose all day. I remember my astrologer he told me that my ultimate mate would take some of my karma for himself to try and help me. I might choose to help him too and take some of his karma on me. To simply help each other. When we were still together, Hazy would talk about using white voodoo to help people. I would always like smile and laugh at him. But now, I remember he had the same symptoms like sinus in the morning, running nose, and headache for 2 months. He asked me "So this is how you feel every morning with your sinus?" For those two months I didn't have to take my medicine and I was free of the symptoms. I felt great. I think he did some white voodoo to help me with my sinus problem. After we broke up I got all the symptoms of sinus back. Deep in my soul I believe I can take his sickness and share my good karma. I do not have to do voodoo. I am healthier than he is because I didn't smoke that long as he did and he will live longer because of me and my healthy karma. It is better to stay on the positive side always."

At seven in the morning I hear this very loud pounding on my door. I wake up and go to the door and see two officers in FBI jackets. Amadeus wakes up and comes to open the door with me.

"Are you Kamila Knapik? We need to talk to you and your son Amadeus in the Tampa FBI office. We like you to go with us there now."

"Yes sir. We will be ready in 15 minutes. Please come inside and wait in the living room. If may I ask, what reason you want us to go with you?"

"We have recorded some of your conversations. We want you to explain them to us."

"But of course."

"You can have breakfast at the FBI office."

"OK. Amadeus go put some clothes on and hurry."

The car ride took 25 minutes. Nobody said anything. it was total silence in the car. Amadeus looked out the window and we held hands throughout the ride.

"Don't worry son, everything will be just fine. I promise." I touched his beautiful hair and held his head next to my chest. "Oh my God, Amadeus" I started talking to him telepathically. He responded to me. "Mommy, don't worry. Like you said, everything will be just fine. We shall not fear." That was a great relief that he knew they couldn't harm me or my son. I could actually hear him mentally.

The ride over the Howard Franklin Bridge to Tampa was unexpectedly very excited. Small three water tornados showed up spinning around each other from both sides of the bridge. Very spectacular and very unusual. At the same time, we saw maybe 30 dolphins on each side of the bridge jumping and racing next to our car. Mother Nature was telling us that something big was about to happen. I could feel the confusion emanating from both of the officers. They didn't know what to think of this situation, but they continued forward, no matter what was happening outside. Amadeus smiled at me. He said "Look, dolphin's mommy. I love dolphins." I smiled back at him and kiss his forehead.

When we got to the FBI office, the officers took us to separate rooms. This made me upset that I couldn't see him. What did the FBI want from a 5 year old boy? They sat me down and showed me a video of Amadeus's room. The video showed Amadeus levitating for about 10 minutes in his bedroom.

"As you suspected, we have been watching and listen to you for a while now. Actually since you applied to FBI agent position although we offered you several great positions, you never took them and we became suspicious also of your alien ex-boyfriend."

I didn't know what to think or what to say. He continued, "We will protect your son. We recommend that you enroll him in the best school in the country for children with his abilities. This school is in Washington D.C. and he can live there during the week. You will be able to see him on the weekends. We also want to give you a job in the same town. I think this is a great opportunity for you both, don't you?"

"Yes, I think the same thing, but I don't like that I wouldn't be able to live and see Amadeus every day. I want him all the time with me."

"He needs to spend more time with kids like him. We need him to learn and explore his capabilities. This small separation is really necessary to reduce his reliance on you. You are ready for this separation, it is good for everybody. We don't really understand children with these powers yet, so we need to have them under close watch. You can trust us, you know that."

He tried to be polite but I felt my blood pressure is going up. I was mad thinking about them taking my son away from me against my will. I could feel in my whole body that something wasn't right.

"I appreciate the job offer. Working for the FBI has been my dream for many years now. But I really don't like idea of separating from my son. This is not my choice and I do not approve it!" I said this very calmly but confidently.

The agent touched me again. I really don't like to be touched, particularly by strangers. This time he grabbed my hand real hard and put his face right to my nose "Listen you little Pollack stripper. We will do whatever we want to do with you. You can actually suck my balls right now. Let me give you some sex love here in this office. Otherwise we are just wasting our precious time."

I didn't push him away, somehow my hand slipped out of his grip, like I float away. I didn't even realize that I had started to levitate away from him. I was up in the air above them now.

The officers started to freak out. I could see the fear in their eyes. They both tried to jump at me to pull me down. But something strange happened. A pink bubble surrounded me for protection. The agents could no longer touch me; the pink bubble was an energy field that protected me.

The officer shouted "What tricks! Do you have more?"

"I really don't know, but I know I don't want to hurt you. Let me and my son go now. You have no right to hold us here against our will."

The officer that shouted at me came closer, this time he spoke softly and slowly "You're right, we cannot hold you like prisoners. You have done nothing wrong so far, but you and your son are freaks of nature. Be aware that we are watching you, so you cannot really run away anyway. We know everything about you and your little boy."

The pink bubble was still around me, protecting me all this time. I floated to the other room where Amadeus was waiting for me. He gave me a warm smile and Amadeus grabbed my hand and came into my pink bubble. It was like he entered my space and we floated towards the main door together. I think it was my love for him that let him enter my pink bubble.

The pink bubble disappeared when we left the building as we started walking away. A car was waiting for us, a different officer opened the door with a big smile and said "Please come inside and sit down." This officer had a pink aura. I knew then I could trust him and talk to him. He said to me very politely "I am very sorry Kamila, that they scared you in there. This was part of the test we perform on new people to see their abilities and response. There are more and more people like your family. We just want to understand, why some people are able or unable, to perform electrical frequencies of color radio waves speed. We don't understand how some people are able to do this while other people are not. If you could help us to understand more, we would be highly appreciative. Here is my card and please call me any time of the day or night if you change your mind."

"Well, thank you." I said, "but I really don't know about it that much."

He continued, "As far we know, strong emotions trigger these abilities. We actually planned this whole test to see if you could perform the same way as you saw Amadeus did in the video. And it did work; your fear activated your abilities. Please keep us informed on any new changes or new abilities. We will be watching you from a distance, so please don't fear us. We just want to understand why there are more and more people like you."

The driver took us home. We were still hungry but I felt calm, not angry or scared at all. Actually I felt very powerful. We ate breakfast and I let my beloved son Amadeus stay home from school. We need to gather our energy after an eventful morning. Amadeus looked at me and gave me a big smile

"I love you mommy. Don't worry; everything is going to be just fine."

"Amadeus, I know it is going to be like this for always now. This weird stuff has been happening to me for years now. But levitating, this craziness is new."

"Mommy, it's not crazy, it's natural."

"This is brand new to me. Why, you must have been levitating for a while now. I don't know what we will do with these powers and how can we use it for good?"

"Well, you control it, so just play with the energy a little bit. Control your mind. Your thoughts are your tools mommy."

"But of course, my son. How could I forget that? "I gave my baby boy a big smile, happiness, kisses and hugs.

I thought back on day when I had used my thoughts to change the temperature setting on the AC unit at work. Many scientist try to experiment on human brains, trying to measure whether thoughts are like radio waves, and whether we are able to use our thoughts to control the world around us. I would like to control machines with my thoughts. That would be awesome.

This was the first day in my life where I didn't feel any fear at all. I didn't feel scared of my powers, or my visions, or my spiritual self. I love myself, and I wanted to learn how to do more. I love levitating and that pink protective bubble. Yes, I have to train myself and learn what else I can do.

Oh, I know what I am going to do first. I am going to take Amadeus to my Polish Catholic church here in St. Petersburg and show the priest Gregory what we can do. Father Gregory baptized Amadeus in his church. I called the church office and made an appointment with Father Gregory for the next day. A few years ago a Vatican Astrologer told all the Catholic believers that it was possible that other intelligent beings could live in the universe. And if any of the alien life tried to contact us as Catholics we should support them because they are creation of God too. The Vatican priest said we should love them and accept them, we should be happy that we are not the only children creation of God.

If I can levitate, can I heal myself too? That would be awesome! I want to heal myself and others too. But how do I do that? This is something I must learn.

"Amadeus, my son, tell me. Can you heal yourself and other people?"

"Mommy, yes. I think I can but I haven't actually tried this yet. I am too small and too young for this. When I get bigger, for sure I will try."

Oh great, so you need to get bigger. Well, that's logical. A human brain will grow until a person reaches 26 years, so there is sure to be much that 5 years old is not yet able to do. Even half alien children still need time to grow. I guess I will have to teach myself. I have taken several energy level initiations with Chi, like Reiki 1, 2 and Tai Chi, so perhaps the fundamental techniques are similar to heal and work with energy. I think I need to imagine myself and my aura as a pure, golden light. The next step involves holding on to this pure energy for as long as I can. Then I will imagine sending out this golden light to others to help and heal them. The two first spiritual truths are: 1) You are what you eat 2) you are what you think. Everyone should be able to work towards these truths. We just need to learn how to control ourselves better.

The next day, I took Amadeus after school to see Father Gregory. He was so pleased to see us both. He is really a nice sweet guy and I have known him now for 8 years. He always remembers me. Polish community is small here in St Petersburg. "Father Gregory please do not be scared. Amadeus and I want to show you something. I really need your help." Amadeus and I started to levitate in front of him. Father Gregory literally jumped out of his chair, looking at us as if he was terrified. He took out his Jesus cross and pointed at us. "Father we are not evil. Do you think this flying is evil?"

Amadeus and I came down and sat at the table. I didn't want to freak out the priest more so he wouldn't have heart attack. Nevertheless, I told him about everything that had been happening to me. I told him all about the visit by the FBI and their school for Amadeus and of course about aliens mixing with humans.

Father Gregory said "Kamila, please just pray to Jesus, come every Sunday for mass. I bless you both. But please don't show this new flying ability to other people. We could try to get an exorcist for both of you, but since you claim this from alien DNA and not a lost spirit that has taken over your body, then an exorcist would not be helpful. Really, I think I need to consider your truth. I have read hundreds of books, and I believe it's possible for the human body to perform acts of Jesus. Yes, Jesus said we will be capable of doing things as he did. So we have to keep calm and do good. We have been given so much already, we need to always try more and be good no matter what our abilities. Thank you Lord."

"Father, I know that. I know also about the First Council of Nicaea in 325 AD. I know about how Jesus had women priestesses but the church expelled them that year. I will not let you think that you can actually control me just because you are the male priest. I am a very strong woman, and I can deliver a message of spirit and strength to all women. We can become priestesses too. Men are not in charge of our lives anymore and they do not have the power to tell us what to do. The sexes are free and equal to each other."

He looked so confused. I thought that maybe Amadeus and I should just walk away. Our flying and my message of feminine strength were just too much information for him to process in one day. "Father, I came here today because of I would like to pursue my life mission of sharing the golden light with the world. I hope that I can get your blessing and that we will continue to see you."

He smiled when we walked away. I felt like I have to do something more. Now that I had visited Father Gregory from the Catholic Church, I thought that perhaps I should visit the Scientology Church to get their opinion on my new abilities. I live near to the biggest Scientology Church in USA with their headquarters in Clearwater Florida. Yes, I liked that idea, so I called and made an appointment to visit a person at the Scientology Church for tomorrow. I needed to go there since they already believed in Jesus and aliens. I know a few Scientologist and they truly help people get back on their feet. However, if you become a Scientologist they want 30% of your income or something like that. That is a lot of money. Other American churches they want about 15%-20% of your income. This seems like a strange American tradition because in Europe, the Catholic Church they don't say anything about suggested or required amounts of income donations. All they say is that you should give as much you can and when you can. I like this better because there is no pressure for money.

The next day, we went there for the meeting. A nice couple greeted us at the door and they give us bottle of water. We went to a private room, where there were about twenty people waiting for us.

"Wow, I guess my public speaking class should become handy now." I said. A woman started speaking, so I started to listen to her.

"We know who you are; we have been watching you and have been guiding you a little. We have a school for children like your son. We will be more than happy if you let him join here with the Scientology Church."

"Wow, you must be really well informed."

"We would like to help you and your son. We know exactly what are you are going through. And we would like to help you."

"Thanks for the offer. I didn't expect that much help. However, I have right now three choices. I can stay here with you guys, go to FBI school for Amadeus, or deal with this on my own. I am confused now; I really don't know where to go next. Since everybody wants to help me, maybe I should try you first." Given that it had taken them nine years of letters to get me here, they were really persistent Americans. "You are very devoted. I have to say that I find your view of Jesus interesting. Actually, I want to believe that Jesus was an alien too. Certainly he wasn't from planet Earth. That, you don't have to convince me. It makes it easier"

"Yes, we know that. But still we will like to show you some of our lectures." The woman said.

"Oh yes. I'd like to see them. Do you have one with Tom Cruise by chance? I will like to watch that one first." She stepped out further from me and shouted out to all of us. "On the ego uppermost trip, where ego is confronting the actual knowledge of the future, we recommend to humble ourselves to the limit of join partnerships—relationships. Where we know, we will be assured about not being correct all the time. Although, there are gifted people, and what is happening to them happens not by conscious choice. They talk about those kinds of people in Bible, they all should be humble and peaceful, not money and power driven."

"I think I know something about this. I am not mad or crazy. I am not a criminal. I am not evil. I am a golden light! I am free. You all cannot touch me. I will put myself in pink bubble. Do you want to see?"

"Oh yes, please demonstrate."

I don't know how I did it; I think was just my will power that controlled my thoughts. It is like I command myself to perform and then it just happened—a big, strong, and very pink bubble appeared. I filled the whole room with this pink energy. The whole room became protected and everyone in the room told me they actually felt my protection in this pink force. I wonder if anybody from outside the bubble could get inside. I had never tried that with anyone, except with Amadeus. I was impressed by myself that I could command this big, protective, healing, energy. I thought, YES I would like to heal people, I would like to heal myself. That would be wonderful.

"The FBI claims, there are more people like me and Amadeus. He is a half god, a half alien himself. But I have a question for you, since you know a lot about aliens. Why they haven't shown themselves yet?"

"Well, we think the people are not ready for them to come back yet. But look at you, Kamila. You are a live example of the change that is coming soon to this planet. We are all about to be able to do what you and your son are already doing. Imagine the consequences and life changes for better."

"I know, this is what I hope for too. Nothing but good will and love will let you fly."

"Can you move objects and control machines?"

"Still working on that one. I did change the Air Conditioner setting and temperature just with my thoughts, but that happened just one time."

"Wow, I imagine I can only control TV or home supplies. Awesome but different."

"Yes, I know. Different. Usually people are afraid of what is different and not understood. But once you understand, you cannot go back. So there is nothing to fear, nothing but yourself. I like this statement very much. It means that I swallowed my fear. I ate it. It's all good now. Nothing to fear of! Nothing to fear for! I am free at last."

"Kamila, hi there. We can actually hear you. We know for certain, you need at least one partner. And you need to be supported and protected by him. Someone who can absolutely understand you and protect you and your son."

"Oh yes, you're right. I already forgot about this problem, that According to the old world, I might be considered crazy or evil. Thanks for remanding me; I was so high with my happiness I could almost float away . . ."

"We are here for you, anytime, if you need us. Please do not hesitate to come over or call. We will support you in all potential ways for a peaceful future. Please stay in contact. We will like to see and hear more sharing from you both."

We went home after this. It was such an emotional day again. Is it going to be like this all the time now? I can handle this so far. We haven't seen any of lectures by Tom Cruise though, which is too bad. But today was a happy day, so pink, so flower like almost fruity. Mmmm like a pink, pink forest.

Oh yes, I understand now why I was able to project the pink energy throughout the whole room. I had seen that once before, during my yoga teacher training course in France. The professor of Siddhi powers turned the whole classroom pink; filling it with a pink energy was coming from him. Now I think he did that because he wanted to protect us, provide shield so nobody could hear or locate us. I was the only one who could answer yes to all of his questions. He knew I had strong Siddhi powers then.

This feels so good, like a constant orgasm. I find myself having sexual fantasies with Hazy like all the time. In my dreams he can give me a constant orgasm from his touch. I did achieve bliss thru transcendental meditation and tantric sex. Ha-ha. I did it both ways.

So what is next? Mind control. Awesome. Like Angel from Las Vegas. He can levitate on his shows. I wish I could meet him and see his show. Like Blue Krishna Hindu God, he was flying all the time in Mahabharata. Flying aliens five thousand years *later, not fighting and not bloody this time, but bringing more peace to come.*

Chapter 8
Love will make you fly

I feel like Hazy is going to show up today. I want this so badly. I feel he is going to come to my house, because this would be the best place for us to meet after so long. We could have wild, wild sex right away. Oh yes, I can't wait for this. I want to see that porn movie he made a long time ago. It is supposed to be what he really likes in sex. Like he could not tell me or show me before . . . Suddenly I hear somebody knocking at the door. Banging really hard like last time. OMG is it Hazy? I went to look and there he was standing, tall and proud as always. Hazy, my Hazy. This is him, right at my door. My feelings were right, wasn't I just thinking about him? I open the door, he walked in and he hugged me so hard. Oh his strong big hugs, I missed them so much.

"I hear that you really need a partner, who knows all your secrets and will protect you all the time. Hey baby love, darling this is me. I am here to protect you and Amadeus."

"Yes my love, I really need you right now and your support in everything I do. I feel so happy and safe again with you here."

"I have to tell you" he continued," I realized that you have been telling me truth all the time. I just needed to protect you from the crazy court case and your crazy ex-boyfriend. Yes, I have been watching you and listened to your phone. I know you know this but I have to tell you this myself. I posted some of our sex videos on YouTube too, to get some attention for my court case. And it did work, we won. We got the building back and the money."

"Good for you Hazy."

"I saw what happened with the FBI, the Catholic Church, and the Scientologists. I need to protect Amadeus and you. I am here for you. I want to be always with you baby. I want to have family with you and I want to get married."

"Hazy, I know honey; you have been telling me this for long time before. Let's do it. I love you too, very much. And I don't want to live without you anymore. Hazy, I think we need to go back to the FBI headquarters, and take their offer. But we need some extra new condition because I want to be with Amadeus everyday not just on the weekends. They cannot just take my son away from me. I will not agree for this; however, I feel obligated as a human to help them to understand more about what is actually happening to me and to other people like me. What is happening to the human race, so many people are changing so quickly, I have a responsibility to support them. I know I need you all the time, I'm so scared to do this alone."

"I know darling, I will be there with you all the time. I was thinking that the FBI would be the best for us too. But before we go to there we need to get married. Because as your husband I have legal rights to protect you and Deus more and even to make some decisions for all of us."

"Ok baby, let's get married. Oh, you always make me so happy. But where is my ring?"

"Well, honey is in my pocket." He took out a beautiful square diamond ring out of his pocket, "Will you marry me my love?"

"Oh yes baby I will marry you!"

We kissed and made love for almost whole night. Of course, it was still filmed on the cameras and he did post this video online again. But what can I say, this is his thing. He doesn't want to change me and accepts me the way I am, so I accept him the way he is. I guess it works both ways. We woke up next day holding tight together and Amadeus came in the morning to our bed.

"Oh mommy, Hazy is back, great I like him."

"Amadeus, Hazy is my fiancé now. Look at my ring, we will get married soon. Are you happy for us?"

"Mommy I love you and Hazy, he is fun. I like when he is chasing me around the house."

"I love you too Amadeus." Hazy said with big smile. Oh what a happy little family.

"Fiancé for short time, we need to get married real fast. Let's go to Vegas tonight, just you and I."

We packed our bags that day, bought couple tickets online, and we were ready to go in only a couple hours. Amadeus stayed with my friend Nene and his best friend Alex for four days. Like a real Americans, we got married in Vegas. It was so beautiful. We got married as soon we got there. The next three days we partied like crazy. And we both know how to party. Just me and him, we were finally a one again. We saw an Angel show. After the show, Hazy was able to get us some private time with him. And there he was, the flying magician speaking to me.

"When I heard you can levitate; I knew right away I had to meet you. It's so nice to meet you Kamila."

"It's my pleasure."

"So can you actually demonstrate your levitation? Please?"

I asked Hazy to hold my hand because I was terrified that it might not work this time. But it did, I started levitating again and Hazy had to let my hand go. I started to spin faster and went way up high. I love this.

"How do you do this?" Angel asked me.

"In truth, I don't know. I just focus my mind and suddenly it's happening. Like I make a command to my brain and it just responds. How do you do your flying?" I asked Angel.

"Exactly the same way. What are you going to do with it? This skill, it can bring you danger in many ways."

"Yes I know, but I have my beloved husband with me and he is devoted to protect me. We were thinking about the FBI's offer, since there are more and more people like us. There, they can study us to better understand our abilities for the good of society. So probably we are going to work with them."

"Well, it was very nice to meet and all the best for you."

"Good luck to you also. Bye."

Hazy and I went for a long walk. I was so happy and fulfilled.

"Hazy, my love thank you for this meeting with Angel. It was very sweet of you to find him for me." I was so impressed with how thoughtful he had been.

"My baby love, let's go to the hotel, we need you get you pregnant so we need to start working on this one."

"Oh yes darling, let's have more fun, fun, fun."

"Let's make some noise. I love it when you scream when I am inside you."

Yes, we did have lots of loud sex. That's what hotels are for, right? The next day we went back to Florida, home sweet home. Amadeus was really happy to see us.

"Mommy I missed you so much, you were gone for so long."

"Oh son, I was only gone for four days. I missed you too."

"Mommy I know you met some people like us, who can levitate right?"

"Yes, but how did you knew that?"

"Oh mommy, I am so connected to you that I can feel you from any distance"

"My beloved son, I remember now, slowly how everything works. How we are all connected through a field of energy. I need to talk to you about our future. There are people from FBI who want to help us. They will put you in special school where I could see you only on the weekends. I don't want that."

"Mommy I don't want that either. You tell them that I can sleep at school only for one night on Mondays. I already know what they do at this special school, and they don't need me more than one night a week. They will agree for it, I can feel it, so mommy don't worry. Ok?"

"Ok, I plan to volunteer and work there too, so I will see you all the time." We did a group hug with Hazy and gave each other big kisses.

Later that day, I called the nice FBI agent. He said that he would come tomorrow to our house to explain the process. They came the next day, but the nice guy wasn't there. Instead four different agents came.

"We have everything ready for you and your family Kamila. You just need to pack only your most beloved stuff. The rest will be provided for you at our final destination."

"What is the rush for? I don't understand."

"We were told that you are ready to go, is that correct?"

"Yes we are ready, but not so fast. Can we leave tomorrow?"

"Everything is ready for transportation. Is 10 am good for you?"

"Yes, it's fine."

Hazy agreed to all these conditions, and we started to pack our most beloved stuff. Hazy, he thinks he knows what will happen. That he can control everything, but he doesn't know what really is involved in a trip like this. Ego is not an option and Hazy doesn't realize this yet. But he will learn soon. We did make sweet love last night, during the sex we both started to levitating within the bubble of pink energy. It was fantastic! Psychic bliss merged with a sexual physical bliss. And of course, a constant orgasmic feeling.

Funny I remember now one of my best girlfriends Kaya had a couple dreams about me like 15 years ago. In her dreams I was levitating, teaching and guiding her how to do it. Look at me now! Her dreams are coming true, I have just started to levitate and my hubby now can levitate with me during sex. I think that both of our Kundalini are now opened. I was just first and his is now opened as well. Hazy took this very naturally, didn't panic at all. Instead he is very excited by it all.

"Kamila, Kamila look at me, I can levitate too. I love it! It's breathtaking. I can't believe I can do this too."

"Hey my love, that's the point, everybody can do this. You just need love. You see how our love make us fly baby. Looks like it's happening as we speak more and more. This is cosmic consciousness and you and I are here to guide people to these new possibilities."

"Oh my darling wife, I am so happy that you have been waiting for me. Thank you for waking me up. I will never let you down. I love you so much and I cannot wait for more fun with this pink bubble."

"Baby I know, I will never let you down either. I love you so much; I hope you know this for good now. And you will never forget this."

Chapter 9
Controlling your energy

*T*he next day, we were all ready and packed for the trip to Washington DC. I don't know why, but we were actually exited to go. The FBI gave us big limo, so we didn't have to take the plane. The trip was long and quiet. The agents didn't talk too much; Hazy and I didn't want to speak to them. The agents were so reserved, that we didn't feel like telling them about what had happened to Hazy last night. Hazy's levitation could wait until DC.

I was really excited to start learning how to use my powers for healing. Along with levitating and telepathy, healing should come too. We took couple stops on the way there, but this one was rather very special. There were some tables very close to the forest where we sat down to eat our lunch. From nowhere, all of a sudden like, hundreds of birds surrounded us and started singing. It was a remarkable sound, somehow it sounded so extravagant. The birds sang until we finished our lunch. Amadeus was so captivated by the sound he didn't even run around like he usually does. Instead, he just sat next to me admiring the energy of loving forest birds.

I wondered about the meaning of the forest birds giving us such a sweet greeting. Did they support us? Did they feel our energy? Was something significant about to happen again? Thinking back to the times when I was sexually confused, I could now see that I was confused about who I was on the energy level. I was confused about my real nature. I realized that I was searching for the deepest truth about my energy. This is something that I have searched my whole life.

At last I have found myself thanks to my beloved son Amadeus. Hazy, he has found himself thanks to me. It's like collective consciousness. I remember learning about a study, done with young monkeys' way back in 1960's. The young monkeys that had been born at zoo started to wash their potatoes before they ate them. This was something they had seen from their trainers, and they adopted the habit as one of their own habits. Meanwhile, the adult monkeys that had been born in the wild never started washing their potatoes. Year after year, at zoos all around the world, young monkeys started to wash their potatoes, spontaneously learning from the humans. Years have passed, and this worldwide collective potato washing phenomenon still isn't understood by scientists. With time, the wild born, adult monkeys did start to their wash potatoes too. The zoo monkeys had finally reached a critical mass, and a new collective consciousness passed over them to the wild forest. So much so, the wild monkeys still living in forests started to wash their sweet potatoes before they ate them. This is the best example of how collective consciousness and critical mass works.

For us humans, only a few people can do what my family of three can do now. I know that soon, very soon, a collective critical mass tipping point would pass over humanity and all of us will be levitating, communicate with telepathy, and who knows what more. Hazy's psychic activation happened because we are so much in love and our love is connected throughout space and time. Even from a far distance he knows how I feel and I feel the same about him. I wondered if perhaps he could activate his mother and I could activate my family and friends. If they are willing to open their mind and believe, our love is strong enough to share and build our collective energy. Of course, we must not fear. That is why those birds at forest, singing their beautiful song to us, sang in happiness celebrating our pure energy of love.

Finally we arrive at our destination. As I suspected, the FBI school was located in the forest, outside of DC. It had a beautiful and spacious location. The school building was extremely large with a modern architectural concrete and steel design. I really liked how it looks from the outside. Flowers and fruit trees were everywhere, like a huge garden. I love it, and thought to myself, "So far so good." A beautiful door made from steel, shaped of apple tree lead into the building. The door opened, seeming to float apart right before us, and we saw this attractive little old lady waiting for us.

She spoke very gently, almost like a whisper. In my mind almost like an echo, I could also hear her "Welcome. We are very pleased to have you all here. My name is Veronica. I have lived here for the past ten years. I am a teacher for the little ones and adviser for the agents. In addition, I am a director of this school. Please do not fear anything here. You are completely safe and protected here. You are free to walk through the entire property as you please, but I will give you a more formal tour tomorrow. Kamila, I know that you just succeeded in activating Hazy, you two and Amadeus stay here while the other newcomers get settled. That way we can speak and can let you know what to do tomorrow. Ok?"

"Great Veronica", Hazy said, "but how did you knew that?"

"Well, we still had cameras at your home remember? I also knew your family was coming here. To prepare for your arrival, I watched you on the surveillance videos. I also reached out my energy to connect to your energy, this way information about your progress comes to me naturally. Right after you wake up, your body is particularly sensitive and sends up massive amounts of pink love energy."

"Oh, so this is what I feel in the morning."

"I know you must be very tired. I will show you to your rooms. Please, feel at home, and we will start fresh tomorrow. Ok?"

Veronica showed us to our very own small cottage with two bedrooms. It was located right at the front of the property. Dozens of little cottages were spread around the school property and I guessed that more than 500 people could easily live on the grounds at one time. It looked like a little village.

Relaxing from the long trip, we all took showers and quietly ate the dinner prepared for us. As it wasn't dark when we finished, we decided to go for a walk around the school and see the whole community. We saw a lake with some boats moored to a dock, a tennis court, and several different playgrounds for kids, pools and a gigantic open field for other sports. We were really impressed and thought it looked like the perfect resort for a family vacation. Hazy and I wondered how long they would let us stay here. So far, we did like it very much.

"I could actually live here, what do you think Hazy?"

"So far so good, but let's not get carried away and see what they have to offer to us first."

"Ok baby."

We woke up next day and went for breakfast in the school hall. Wow, there were so many kids running around, and many kids passing us by were singing. Everybody was extremely nice and greeted us happily. Some of the kids started singing, "Amadeus, Amadeus, rock me Amadeus." We were little bit overwhelmed by this greeting and their enthusiasm for Amadeus to join the school.

After breakfast Veronica took us to her office and gave us more information. "Well, since both of you guys have already activated your powers through unconditional love, we would like to invite you to stay here. That way you can stay with Amadeus and don't have to worry about anything."

"Oh this is wonderful, we love the property and I couldn't leave Amadeus based on the terms that the agents had previously told us"

"We understand this. A mom needs to be near her children, but we need all the kids together. As you might know by now, our work is based on critical mass and collective consciousness, to help wake up others like you. Amadeus is so strong and he can help so many others, so it is critical for the kids to stay together at least at the beginning like right now."

"I understand this, but I will not leave my son alone here for five days a week. That is not an option."

"Of course, Kamila, you and your husband can stay in this cottage as long as you want. If the time comes when you need a bigger house there are plenty fine-looking houses next to our village that you can move to. In the meantime, we need both of you here. You both have things to learn and things to teach others too. Sound good?"

"Yes, yes it does" Hazy said.

"Next," Veronica continued, "I have to tell you, why we are separating ourselves from others in society. This is because we don't want them to panic because of our powers or for them to judge us while we are still learning, developing, and expanding our energy. Given time, they will become exactly the same as us, but right now they have no clue. As a result of that, we have to protect ourselves from people who are not activated yet. We know they will be activated soon, but for now it has to be this way. We can see more and more spontaneous activations, though many people throughout the country still live in fear of their own love and psychic energy. Instead, they prefer to be on their own. Some of them even pretend like nothing happened to them. They live in denial, not wanting to learn about unconditional love or the bliss of the pink bubble of energy.

Some hide and practice their new potential quietly in their homes. Still, these hidden participants contribute their energy to our collective progress and work for the critical mass. However, at this point it's better to stay together. We cannot let anyone come here. The government is actually very supportive of this secret project and we have at least one school like this per state. We choose this school for you, because Amadeus's father comes from a long line of important politicians in this country. Amadeus's father and grandfather are both still politicians, important in the government and supporting our work here. We think that Amadeus will continue his family tradition."

"Of course, as Amadeus's father is a shape shifter, even though Amadeus is only half alien, we hope that he also will gain these abilities. Not all the kids at this school have aliens for their parents. Some of them are 100% humans, just with very high energy levels. But we can talk about shape shifters later. Right now we have a very big surprise for both of you. Let's introduce you to Amadeus's new classmates and teachers."

Veronica led us over to a school. "Like I said, some of the children here are half aliens just like Amadeus. They have very special DNA. Right now, there are almost 6 million shape shifters living in the United States. Of course there a lot of kids too—their powers are related to their love. Most of the kids live at home with their parents. However, some aliens prefer that their children live in our schools for the simple reason that they want to protect their offspring. They want them to evolve naturally. Possibly into shape shifters, not in regular school but here where they are safe and others know and understand what they are going through. Some parents, those who have activated their powers, live here. Other parents live close by and come here regularly for visits. Ok, now let's go to Amadeus. But I have to say, I love his name the one who loves God and Deus for short the God, and Kamilah, the perfect one—What great family names. Inspired choices!"

We introduce Amadeus to his new friends and he was so happy to meet them all. Amadeus told me he was so happy to come here. Already he had learned that he could communicate telepathically with most of the children. Some of the children he had telepathically communicated with for some time. They already knew each other through their minds! This was so exciting for him. Now they were able to finally meet, person to person for the first time. There was like 60 kids around his age. All of them were laughing, happily playing and singing.

Veronica suggested that we leave him there among the kids and teachers. She wanted to show us the rest of the school building. It had seven floors. On each floor were classrooms devoted to a different age group. Students were taught subjects such as the art of mind control and Veronica pointed out the steel decorations dispersed through the building that had been shaped by the students' minds. The kids were actually bending the metals with their thoughts, using their creative instinct to perfect their mental control skills. Although many of these classes were for the young children, Veronica assured Hazy and I that we could both take this class to perfect our own skills in mind control.

I asked Veronica "What do you want to achieve by building up our mind control abilities? How likely are we to learn how to do this? We both want to learn more, however, these strong powers make us nervous."

Veronica responded, "Yes, learning these skills is why you have been invited to stay here. We want to teach you first so you can soon teach others in the future."

"Great! I love the thought of learning about art and metal. I'm ready to learn this right now". Hazy said with his beautiful smile on.

"Hold your horses, we have tons to learn before you begin this class. You need to learn first how to control your own energy. However, I am so happy to see you so excited."

"First of all we need to teach you how to defend and protect yourself with the pink bubble. We do not accept violence or attacks here. Only in extreme situations where you might need to protect yourself. But the defense training only happens at the six and seven levels. Only after you have developed enough control and demonstrated your abilities for good. Only then are most trusted allowed to begin the defense training. Before that, most of the time we teach people how to control machines with our thoughts. And of course, we encourage and help you develop your basic love of yourself and of others. Telepathically, we are all one, after all. Healing is also a big part of the training here. These classes will only begin after you have passed the first five levels. Only some students can reach this because it involves much love, energy, devotion, and a massive change in life style."

"That is fantastic! I want to learn how to heal people."

"I thought that you might want that Kamila, we can start first thing tomorrow morning. Tomorrow is going to be big day for both of you."

Everything that Veronica told us, sounded great to me. Already I could feel a sweet force of expectant energy come all over me.

When Amadeus came back to our cottage after his day at school, the first thing he said was, "Mommy, mommy, I love this place. All kids are like me! I don't have to pretend anymore that I don't know stuff. Lots of the kids have parents which are aliens, and some kids, their parents don't live here. Instead, if their alien parents have big responsible careers in the government, the parents only visit on the weekends. Some of the kids told me that I have the greatest mom in the whole world because you are here with me all the time. Well, I knew that already, but I'm so happy that I can live here and that you can stay here. Oh mommy I am so happy! The kids, told me also that most humans' mothers, they don't understand their children's abilities, so give their kids to exorcists or mental hospitals to cure them of their powers.

"Oh my beloved son, I was praying for a diamond baby like you for ten years. I love you and will never leave you alone. I will die and kill for you. Do you understand?"

We all went to bed early that night. We were extremely tired and overexcited from all the emotions of hope, joy, and expectations flowing through us. Hazy was inspired, and my brand new hubby introduced me new sex positions while we both levitated. During earth bound sex, these positions never were possible before. You can only imagine, but I wondered whether the astronauts in space ever had sex and knew these feelings.

The next morning Veronica took us to the top floor of the school building. We entered a very private room. I gasped when I saw Charlie, Amadeus' father, waiting for us there. This Charlie was over 6.6 feet tall and looked to be about 400 pounds now.

"Hello to you all. Nice to see you. Kamila, I am glad that you are finally happy with Hazy. I still wish that you wanted us to be together, but I cannot change that he is the one you want. My broken heart and alcohol has given me kidney cancer. Yes, even we aliens can get sick too, when we lose access to unconditional love. But you, Kamilah outgrew me, and I need your powers to heal me. Please."

Veronica looked me and she said, "Yes, you have to try at least. Believe in the unconditional love for your son and Amadeus' love for his father. This will guide you. You already know how to heal people. You took Reiki as I remember, right?"

"Yes I did, but I never tried to heal someone this sick before. Reiki involved just sending energy, not like real healing.

Veronica looked me deep down into my eyes, staring so deep and unblinking that she almost hypnotized me. She did not speak with her mouth this time. Instead, I could hear her voice telepathically in my mind. "This is your highest test that you ever faced; you must push forward with your abilities."

"Hazy, did you hear that my love? Did you hear what Veronica just said?"

"No, what are you talking about darling."

"Oh, Veronica just spoke to me in my mind and I heard her voice. She said that I have to do this because this is my most important test."

"Well, than do it honey."

I asked Hazy and Veronica to take a step back from Charlie, so only he could absorb my healing energy. I came closer to him as he was sat on the chair and I situate myself behind him. I touched his shoulders and lower back with my opened hands. I opened my heart and I closed my eyes. I thought of forgiveness, unconditional love, and sent my gold energy to heal him. In my mind's eye, I could see his anger splattered in blood red energy with a black spot on his kidney. The red and black energy disappeared, washed away by my rays of golden light. Then I saw all different colors in his aura growing, spreading, and moving faster and faster all over him. I opened my eyes, and the whole room was filled with rainbow colors and golden light. I could tell that he already could feel so much better; his body was healing on the energy level at first. In my mind's eye, I could see his body healing inside. I had a vision pinpointed like a microscope. When his kidney changed to his natural colors, I stopped my golden rays of light.

I turned to Veronica and Hazy, "Did you guys see that?"

Their eyes where small and still shiny, like they had been blinded by the light. "Yes we did." They both answered smiling.

Charlie stood up and hugged me right there. "Thank you so much, I always believed in you, that you can do it. So now I can show you what you always wanted to see without any distractions. Sit next to your husband and hold his hand."

I sat down beside Hazy. Charlie stood right in front of us. Slowly, his body and face started changing shape. A wave of energy started moving around him. Charlie changed into a face and body that I recognized. It was his first body in which I had met him in Geneva. Charlie became Peter body again, right there in front of us.

"I know now" he said, "You have so much power and connection to the Earth than I thought at first you should understand. Please forgive me for any hurt that I may have given to you. I can tell that your marriage is filled with love and I wish you both all the best. I will be there for Amadeus anytime he needs me. Aliens and humans, we are almost the same now because human body came to perfection. Therefore we can easily shape shift into. Kamila, you are leading the way, but we cannot force others to change. People have to wake up by themselves; otherwise they will think that we are bad aliens that are only out to control humans with our mind. That is exactly what we don't want. We can help just a little by little, behind the curtain with this school, but you, humans, have to do the work. We can show you all the books and tools but you all need to practice, experience, and learn by yourselves.

Now that you have healed me Kamila, I have to go back to Bern Switzerland. There is work I must do in Africa and India, for the Swiss government. My time as Charlie is done, and I know that you do not need me anymore. Hazy will be a good protector for you and I know I can trust my beloved son Amadeus with him. Otherwise I would not leave you here alone. Now I want to see Amadeus. I will like to go and see him now."

We all went to Amadeus classroom. And guess what, as soon as we walked in Amadeus ran into Peter's arms like he knew who he was. Amadeus must have recognized his soul even though he had never seen his dad in this particular body. Hazy and I went to our cottage, while Amadeus went with Peter to the park for some quality daddy and son time.

"Amadeus, listen to me now. As your father I will always protect you; even though we have just reunited, I have to leave for a little while. You must remember everything I taught you for all these five years, especially the defense training. However, you must not show or tell anyone about this defense energy level. Do you understand my son?"

"Yes, father."

"You are still too young for this secret energy use, I have no choice but to teach you for your own protection, but you must keep it to yourself. You can only use it if your mommy is in danger. Watch out for Hazy especially. You may need to use your fighting powers against him if he tries to harm your mommy. Ok? We don't know yet how he is going to use his pink bubble. You see your mother is doing great job with healing now, the highest energy level of unconditional love. But we don't know how he will use his powers yet. He also had some ego issues before, so his love might not be deeply true. Therefore you have to watch him, and look after your mommy. Remember though, you are only to use your fighting powers for defense, and then only when you absolutely have to."

"Ok dad. I am not scared any longer. Living here is fun. I just hope to see you more often."

"Don't worry Deus; I will always see you once a week, just like before. Just don't talk to anybody about this. Ok? Not even with your mother. Your mom and the others are not ready for this advance energy, like you are. We cannot introduce them to this yet. Do you understand?"

"Yes, dad I do. I miss you already."

"Well, I'll see you next week son. And remember, your mother loves you the most. She will do her utmost to protect you, so you have to do the same to protect her. Especially when I am not here."

"Father, I understand now how to use attack energy. Don't worry, you taught me well."

Amadeus went back to his class and Peter left the golden village without a goodbye. But that's ok; he isn't good with goodbyes. Amadeus kept all the secrets his father told him and they continued to meet once a week. I only found out later *when I got to seventh level of energy initiation. But this is another story.*

At this higher level Hazy was very impressed by my new healing abilities. He asked me to teach him too so we could heal his mother. Of course, I said yes. The truth about healing is the stronger you believe in the healing process, the work almost gets done by itself. The energy around us responds to the human impulse of love. Love is always the strongest force.

Chapter 10
Priestess Kamilah

With Hazy, we make a decision to leave Amadeus here for couple days and return to Florida to heal Hazy's mom. After this, we plan to go to Europe to heal my mother, but Amadeus will go with us for the second trip to Europe. On the way home to Florida, we took a plane rather than the limo that originally brought us here. I was hoping that things would be easier with Hazy's mom since now we were married. I love my husband very much so she should start accepting me now. When we got back to town, she was in a small gallery exhibition. When we got there, she smiled at us. But something was wrong with one of her eyes. Its color had changed to white.

There were a lot of people in the gallery. We didn't have a chance to tell her about our new talents since our transformation had only happened like one week ago. Nor had we told her that we had gotten married. For that reason, I wanted to give her show. I asked Hazy to trust me and let me talk to her first. I have my back covered by Hazy so everything should be fine.

I told him that I had to get her emotions going first so she can see why she is sick and why she was going blind. "Honey my love, I trust you with my life and with my mother life too. I know you won't disappoint me." "Hazy, just watch and fly with me and do exactly everything like me if you want to heal her. Ok?"

"Yes, you're my wife and I trust you. Ok baby let's crash this party and heal my mom."

We approach Hazy's mom with flowers. She smiled when she saw this. I said to her, "Charlotte, we got married last week. I'm sorry that we did it behind your back but that was Hazy's decision to rush. We love each other very much."

"Hazy, good for you. Did you sign the prenuptial agreement?"

"No mother, we did not"

"Haven't you learned anything from my life experience? She is going to take all your money."

"Mom, it's not like this." I said. I realized that all the people in the gallery were looking at us. "Charlotte, look at us, see what our love can do."

I grabbed Hazy's hand and we started to levitate. Instead of two pink bubbles we become one big pink bubble of energy. All the people in the gallery were amazed. Compared to the art, our levitation and pink force were pretty cool. Hazy's mom knew right away what was going on and she started to cry.

I said to her, "Mother, do you want me to try to heal you? My powers have grown."

"Yes, yes, I do."

"But mother, you need to know at first why this sickness came to you"

"I know, you don't have to tell me. My sickness is from my anger, my fear, blame and my broken heart. I need to trust people and if you forgive me, I will give you my blessings."

"Please forgive me and I give you my blessings too, Mother."

Hazy and I came down from our pink cloud to heal Charlotte. I asked her to sit down and we both put our hands on her. As we started the procedure the whole room started to fill up with different colors of energy. Everybody was standing still and watching. Hazy and I created a golden and white light to start the healing process. The people didn't panic, so that was nice. After ten minutes the healing was all done. Mother gave us big smile.

"I am so sorry I didn't believe in you Kamila. That was only my fears speaking for me, my instinct to protect my only child from all the bad things that had happened to me."

"Mother, I knew that all along, I was just hoping that we could reach this happy day today together. And here we are today. Would you like to levitate with us mother?"

"Oh girl, bring it on."

We both grabbed her, Hazy took his mother from one side, and I went to the other. Up we started to levitate, and guess what happened? She created out her own pink bubble! All of a sudden, she let go of our hands and started to levitate all by herself. Everybody in the gallery started clapping, some people even screamed—this is the best show ever.

The unexpected continued to happen. The people who were cheering the loudest suddenly started to create their own pink bubbles and levitated up to Hazy, Charlotte and I. Then all the people in the whole room started to create flying pink bubbles.

I think the critical mass is building and taking us closer to the tipping point. Hazy and I told them all about the FBI and Amadeus's school. Of course we told them all about the shape shifters too. We gave them the contacts numbers to the FBI agents if they need help. But I didn't want to stay there too long. It wasn't my place to teach them and I wanted to go back to my son and prepare for our trip to Europe.

Before we left St Petersburg, Hazy and I took mother and her boyfriend Lee to a nice restaurant for dinner. As soon as we all sat down to the table, Lee got upset when he realized that he had been the only one who hadn't created the pink bubble in the gallery. He asked me why.

"Well, Lee, do you remember when one day Charlotte and Hazy were in his bedroom talking business and you and I were sitting in living room waiting for them to finish?"

"Yes, I do remember."

"You hushed me, when I had tried to start a polite conversation with you. I think you didn't know how to connect to me. You have to try to connect to Charlotte and hopefully she will help you to create your pink bubble."

Dinner went just fine. We were all happy and giggling all the time. The next morning, Hazy and I took a flight back to DC. We met Veronica at the airport and quickly told her what had happened in Florida. She was amazed; she said that she never heard about this kind of spontaneous group opening before. Veronica also told us that only a few people from our group in DC had developed so strong healing power as I had done in one week. I guess I am very strong willed and powerful after all.

The next day, with Amadeus in hand, all three of us flew off to Berlin, Germany. After the seven hours flight, we finally landed in Berlin where my beloved first cousin Michael was waiting for us. We still had a 1.5 hour drive to Szczecin, the city of the Pomeranian Princess and where my mother lived. We arrive at my mother's house and she was so happy to see us all. Suddenly, just as in Florida, pink bubbles and flying started to spontaneously happen again. We weren't even doing it on purpose. My close family was there, along with my auntie Yolanda, my uncle Waldemar, and my second cousin Peter. They panicked a little at first. No one expected this! But soon we were all laughing. My family has always been very spiritual so it didn't take too long to explain their transformation. They already knew about auras and healing energies, because all of them had studied Reiki like I had done.

My uncle was so impressed that the next day, he brought 30 people to his house for Hazy and I to teach and heal them. Again we activated everyone's pink bubble. It was so cute, so funny, so spiritual, and so joyous. Every day, more and more people kept coming to my uncle house wanted to be healed and activated.

Of course we could have said no, as commanding these energies started to be exhausting. I was so worried. I called Veronica not knowing what I should do. Veronica said that the critical mass might top over soon and since the global wakening had started to happen. Needing a break, we went to Geneva, Switzerland, just for a week to see Amadeus' Godmother, Angelica. Even here, all the same things started happening. Pink bubbles of unconditional love floated around my closest friends. After three weeks of this, we were simply exhausted and ready to come home. This time, Washington, DC would be our new home.

Veronica had told me that a surprise was waiting for us in

Washington. We were so excited to see what it was this time. Amadeus was very happy to return to all his new friends. But when we got home, despite our excitement, we slept for a long time.

Next morning right after breakfast, Veronica took Hazy and I to a special room on the seventh floor. All of a sudden, Veronica's body shifted to alien a gray-blue. She started to talk to me telepathically. I could hear her very well. I don't know if Hazy could hear her, but I think he did too.

"I have a supreme pleasure to introduce you to our Queen Mother from our planet. She will like to meet you right now. Are you ready to meet her?"

"Yes, I am ready."

Out of nowhere she appeared, the Queen Mother of the aliens' supreme species, right there in front of me. She looked almost like Veronica's alien body, but her head was bigger and she had pale white skin with blue, green and purple black eyes.

She spoke to me, "I am so proud of you Kamilah, you are the perfect one, just as you were intended to be. You have already done great work. Your healing powers came quickly and are very strong. Wherever you go, you now bring people to true love and activate their pink bubbles."

"But I have no clue how all this is happening."

"Yes, but we do know how. You are very strong, your will and your heart will light up the whole universe only if you want. We just wish everybody would be so strong and open like you. By the way, congratulations guys, you are pregnant!"

In the same moment we heard a loud knocking at the door. Ms. Jessica, one of the teachers was at the door and she started jumping from happiness and screaming like crazy. "It's happening! It's happening! It's all over the TV news."

We went down to TV room, and there it was, right there all over the main channels. Live CNN cameras showing Chicago, NYC, Los Angeles, Rome, Paris, Berlin, London, India and

China. People everywhere were creating their pink bubbles one after another and starting to fly. Everybody was so happy levitating and experiencing this natural phenomenon. No panic at all, just bliss. More and more people were jumping and levitating up high in the air.

The Queen Mother turned to me and said, "You see Kamilah; it has started, but this is only level one. You are already up to the fifth level. Where there are seven levels as you know. You have big responsibility in front of you to guide and teach others. We can take everyone over from this beginning up to level seven."

"But how do I do that?"

"Don't worry we will guide you and people will open up spontaneously. You will have tons of help. You have Hazy next to you. He is already on level three. Remember there are many people like you. Go now to Amadeus and enjoy your time with him. In soon future, you will have to travel a lot and teach many people. And yes Hazy, I can hear your question; it's going to be a boy and a girl. Twins."

"Great, I like that already. It was honor to meet you Queen Mother."

"No Kamilah, we have always known each other. It was nice to see you again in this life, Kamilah my priestess."

....

To be continue . . .
Book II 'RETURN OF THE ISIS'